Gift of Revelation

Gift of Revelation

Robert Fleming

www.urbanchristianonline.com

Urban Books, LLC
97 N18th Street
Wyandanch, NY 11798

Gift of Revelation Copyright © 2015 Robert Fleming

ISBN 13: 978-1-60162-693-6
ISBN 10: 1-60162-693-2

First Trade Paperback Printing March 2015
Printed in the United States of America

10 9 8 7 6 5 4 3 2 1

Distributed by Kensington Publishing Corp.
Submit orders to:
Customer Service
400 Hahn Road
Westminster, MD 21157-4627
Phone: 1-800-733-3000
Fax: 1-800-659-2436

Gift of Revelation

A Novel

by

Robert Fleming

"For without are dogs, and sorcerers, and whoremon-
gers, and murderers, and idolaters, and whosoever
loveth and maketh a lie."
—Revelation 22:15

"In the end, we will remember not the words of our
enemies, but the silence of our friends."
—Reverend Martin Luther King, Jr.

DEDICATION

This book is dedicated to the fearless,
selfless medical teams of Doctors Without Borders
(Médecins Sans Frontières), which are attacking suffering
throughout Africa and the rest of the world.

Also, much respect and love to my brother,
Anthony Fleming, who orchestrated the farewell
voyage of our father, Robert Sr.

ACKNOWLEDGMENTS

A book is only as good as the team that produces and supports it.

The patience and editorial skill of Joylynn M. Ross, of Urban Christian, sustained this manuscript through a bit of a difficult family crisis. She shepherded it through rough spots to the finish line of publication.

My thanks goes to Pastor Carol Spor of Saint Paul, Minnesota, who put our family tree on the map. To my extended family, Aunt Mary of Omaha, Michelle, Mercedes, Val, Ethel and Oscar, Vandella, Linda Smith, Hzal (Anthony Fudge), Art Nixon, Russell, Gary Brozek, and Cheryl Woodruff, who saved my life.

To Verta Mae Grosvenor, my mentor and friend. To Troy Johnson, the founder of AALBC.com. And to Thea of Black Christian Book Promo.

1

A NEW LEAF

When we arrived in New York City, I took over my old apartment in Harlem and watched Addie settle into her new surroundings. She was a stranger in a strange land. Everything caught her eye. She marveled over everything. I hadn't wanted to go back to my old life, but I'd been afraid to take on anything else.

No sooner had I got back than the phone rang, and it was word about the death of a mentor, Monsignor Edgar Ryan, a man who had advised me when I was accepted into the seminary. He was ninety-one years old, and I had not seen him for several years. The church had shut him away when they learned he had a touch of senility. Still, the monsignor had snuck calls to me in the middle of the night, talking about the pope and the future of the Catholic Church, abortion, perverted priests, the religious right, baseball, the lure of the tainted Internet, and the missionary life in Africa and the Far East.

"Will you be at the funeral service, Reverend?" one of his aides asked after giving me the address of the location on Staten Island where the church would be celebrating his funeral mass.

"Yes, I'll be there," I said firmly. "Nothing could keep me away." I remembered how the monsignor had welcomed the working poor and immigrants into his parish, teaching tolerance and compassion.

Monsignor Ryan's service presented several problems for the church, since his spiritual history would have to be rewritten to some degree. I wondered if the powers that be were going to sugarcoat his ministry or if they were going to tell the factual version. Some of the truths he had uncovered in his outreach were shameful and embarrassing to the Vatican. That had made him a target, with a bull's-eye on his back. Warts and all, the monsignor had been a regular guy. Yes, I would be there to honor his name and his spiritual work.

I still had not tidied up part of the spare room. This was possibly because I was afraid that I'd find some painful items that had belonged to my late, departed wife, which was exactly what I found behind a few cardboard crates on a shelf. Nothing had prepared me for the pink shoe bag containing a pair of flashy red high heels and a note written in my late wife's hand. It read: *My lack of communication with you is all me. I don't know what's happening inside me. You are and always will be a part of my life. During my silence, I've been reevaluating my membership in the human race, and I have yet to decide if I want to renew it. I love you and cherish you. Never second guess this! Be patient. Please.*

The note brought tears to my eyes, churning up old memories of her and the children. I balled the note up and tossed it against the far wall. Squeezing my eyes shut, I fought down the pain that could overwhelm my heart. I couldn't relive that suffering.

With that settled, I watched Addie befriend one of Dr. Smart's sisters, a hairdresser for the local TV personalities, find a suitable place to live on the West Side of town, talk to area school officials to land a job, and begin her walking tour of Harlem. But she never gave up on me, hoping to persuade me to make a real commitment to her.

"While you're making up your mind, I'm going to occupy my time checking out Harlem," Addie said, just happy to be here and not down South, where all the trouble was.

Only a week after our exodus, we walked along 125th Street, past the crowd of strollers and tourists; past the vendors selling everything from bootleg videotapes to cheap fruit and vegetables purchased from the Hunts Point Market in the Bronx; past the fast-food joints; past zealous churchgoers passing out handbills filled with fire and brimstone; past the Apollo Theater, the Adam Clayton Powell Jr. State Office Building, the Studio Museum, and a dingy White Castle burger place near the famous Hotel Theresa, where Malcolm X had his office and the Cuban revolutionaries Fidel and Che stayed in the fifties.

"How do you like your first slider?" I asked her when she took her first bite of the mini-burger. We had stopped at the White Castle along the way.

She continued chewing the wafer-thin burger, the meat and bread balled up in her cheek. "Good. They're addictive," she finally said.

We had bought a half dozen of them, two large Cokes, and a small bag of chocolate chunk cookies. I loved catering to the kid in her. Everything was so new to her. She loved New York City.

Before we flew away, we never talked about what had happened in Alabama: the consequences of the Prophet Wilks tragedy, Reverend Peck's final sellout, the ruthlessness of the white planters, or the deadly showdown in that desolate field. Whenever I brought it up, she ignored me or switched the subject. She hated anything to do with her rural past; instead, she wanted to concentrate fully on the moment, on the future. And she was right.

In her cramped apartment close to 125th Street, I sat drinking a cup of coffee in the living room while a news announcer on TV spoke about how most low-income students who had good test scores and top grades avoided applying to the best colleges and universities. The white man, who looked like an insurance salesman, noted that this pattern contributed to the growing economic inequality and the suffocating low rate of mobility in poorer areas of the country. He said it like a Rodney Dangerfield wisecrack.

"Clint, I saw this when I taught school down South," Addie said, frowning. "The kids stop believing in themselves. They don't believe they can be successful. When you don't believe in yourself, you stop trying."

"Or you stop applying to the better schools," I added. "That's a shame. Do you think you're going to teach up here? You'd be good at it."

She poured herself a cup of coffee in that tiny space and spoke slowly, as if memorizing a mantra. "Clint, I feel like a fish out of water, but I like it. I like challenges, because you have to go beyond what you are used to. You have to go beyond your comfort zone. I know I'll do all right here."

"Do you regret leaving your hometown?" I asked.

"No. Sooner or later I had to leave," she replied.

Addie was fearless, unrepentant, unapologetic, and unbowed. That was the way I liked her. She believed her life was up to her, within her control, and she had no regrets. None at all.

"What do you require of me?" I asked.

"Honesty. That's all." She sipped the brew.

"What else?" I was fishing.

"Integrity. If you have those things, there is nothing else to ask of a man." She smiled, flashing her dark eyes at me.

We sat down at the kitchen table, drank our coffee, talked about our wants and needs, our dreams and obstacles. She was so different than Terry, my late wife, in her attitudes, her kindness, her forthrightness. She never minced words.

"Clint, when I met you, I didn't know if I liked you or not." She giggled. "I guess you grew on me. I saw how you treated everybody around you, and I knew I liked that."

"Why didn't you like me at first?" I saw how spotless she kept the place. There was not a speck of dust anywhere.

She poured a little cream in her coffee. "You were too quiet. I thought you were hiding something. I like men who talk. You were so closemouthed. I thought you were too darn sure of yourself."

I was embarrassed. There was nothing like seeing yourself in another person's eyes. It was very humbling.

"But my family loved you right off," she said, laughing. "They could tell you were a quality man by the way you treated me. You're always a gentleman. They saw how you held the door for me, pulled out my chair, helped me put on my coat. That counts for something. More men should do things like that."

I looked past her, at the wall that held a photo of her mother, a sepia portrait of the woman in her youth, dressed in a summer dress gently blowing in the wind. It was one of her prized possessions, which she kept dusted and free from the grime emitted by the steady traffic.

"Clint, what are you going to do with yourself?"

I don't know really. "I might go back to my old job."

"And what was that?"

Thinking about my job prospects, I decided I might take a run downtown and see if they wanted a social worker at the welfare department or somebody at the Social Security office. But jobs were as scarce as hen's teeth, and nobody was hiring. The economy was in a slump. It had been stuck in a very deep funk ever since the Bush administration had ruled the roost.

"Were you fired from your last job?" she asked.

"No. I was counseling at my church, but the man who hired me had a problem with me. I don't think I can ever go back there again. The elders at the church would not want me back, and I wouldn't want to go back. I think I must find something new."

Addie nodded. "Yes, get a fresh start."

There was a ray of hope. I'd learned from my mistakes. Dr. Smart made a fool out of me, and the elders were happy to see me gone. They would not forgive me. Nor would they believe in my redemption.

"I was telling my lady friend about you, and she said it's possible to rebuild your name by sheer determination and hard work," Addie volunteered. "They'll overlook your past problems if you keep your nose to the grindstone and focus on your work."

"Are you saying I was a hothead?"

"Not at all. You're putting words in my mouth."

"Then what *are* you saying?" I asked her.

Addie folded her arms over her chest and, with an emphasis on each word, said, "I'm saying you need to forget all about the past and build your future. Sometimes it doesn't matter if you have all kinds of achievements and abilities if you're full of pride."

I protested. "But I'm not like that."

"You're probably not like that," she said, grinning. "But I don't know your ways. I don't know when you get a bit of temper or fuss and fight rather than compromise. I wonder if you get surly and aggressive or want to have your way. I'm waiting for you to show your bad side. Everybody has one, and I want to see yours."

When she finished, I shook my head. "I don't have a bad side. I'm not perfect, but I'm not a monster, either. I'm pretty much an even-keeled person, with no extreme highs or lows."

She looked at me over the edge of her cup. "Well, we'll see. Nobody's that perfect. Everybody has something they need to work on." With that remark, she closed her eyes and shut me out of her vision, out of her nimble mind.

2

FEELING THE CHILL

It was a gray day, overcast with dark clouds, but it was not supposed to rain. And it didn't. Church officials had changed the location of Monsignor Ryan's funeral service from the small church in Staten Island to a much larger one on the East Side of Manhattan, accommodating a much greater number of mourners than the tiny venue out on the outskirts of the city.

Hundreds of people had lined up to see the black hearse carrying the body, some holding flowers and signs of tribute, others shouting their grief at the coffin as it was driven to the mammoth church. Some waved good-bye; others wept. At Monsignor Ryan's church in Staten Island the previous night, there had been a steady line of the faithful who had come to see the body, which had been decked out in the full regalia of a monsignor in good standing. Television segments had shown a group of volunteers, nuns, priests, and other church representatives standing guard, along with a small platoon of cops. Nobody had acted unruly, and the event had gone on without a hitch.

Although I had frequented a number of the city's Catholic cathedrals, I'd never been to St. Jean Baptiste Roman Catholic Church, located a few blocks from Lenox Hill Hospital. It was written about in the newspapers and featured on television. Ornate and imposing, the cathedral was constructed in the shape of a cross, with a huge dome and rows upon rows of pews for worshippers. I stared at the grand organ overhead and marveled at the collection of intricate stained-glass windows, each and every one depicting the Blessed Lord, the Virgin Mary, or scenes from the scriptures.

It was a high honor for the fallen monsignor Ryan to have his funeral mass conducted by the Vatican's assistant secretary of state, Cardinal Enrico Rossi. I sat in the section where the ministers of other faiths were located, between a representative of the Greek Orthodox Church and someone who was a holy man of the Rasta religion, his dreads flowing down onto a bright red outfit.

"Monsignor Ryan welcomed every human being into the spiritual fold, saw the soul of God in every downtrodden man and woman," Cardinal Rossi said. "He saw the possibility of redemption and salvation in every human being. He felt that when divine love had accomplished its mission, this was a reflection of the divine order. Our Lord came into this world to redeem it. Our Lord welcomed death. Most of us who are born see death as a departure, an interruption, an end. Our Lord saw death as His crowning glory, as a passage to the final reunion, as the destination of redemption."

As I looked around while Cardinal Rossi spoke, I noticed three rows of mourners dressed in colorful African robes; nuns in white saris with the distinctive blue outline of the Missionaries of Charity, of the Mother Teresa variety; a row of men in business suits; and a row of Buddhist monks in their customary orange robes.

"Monsignor Ryan understood the commandments of our Blessed Lord," the Cardinal continued. "He reached out over the city to the villages, to the burgs, stretching forth his hands, saying, 'For whosoever shall do the will of my Father, which is in heaven, the same is my brother, my sister, and mother.' Our brother understood there are greater bonds than just those of flesh and blood, namely, the sacred spiritual ties that band together the faithful of the Kingdom."

Some of those in attendance felt uneasy about sitting with such a motley group of unbelievers, but they made a pretense of being comfortable. A nun pointed out the "unfortunates" who were present: three young thugs redeemed from prison; a blind woman; two orphans; a young hooker ravaged by AIDS, who was being assisted by friends; and a disfigured veteran soldier from the Iraqi conflict, who was missing both legs.

Holding his arms aloft, the cardinal adjusted his notes and moved through his eulogy. "Our Blessed Lord completed His work. Monsignor Ryan has completed his work, but all of us have not completed ours. We are not finished. Like our Blessed Lord, Monsignor Ryan gave an example for us to follow, to take up the cross with the purest of hearts and souls and move through this life. He has completed his quest in his physical body, has finished his journey. Like our Blessed Lord, the monsignor has completed sowing the seed, and now we the faithful are preparing for the harvest."

Someone said a loud amen. That was unusual for a solemn Catholic service like this one. Silence was the rule for such services.

"The monsignor knew he had to walk beside the faithful until it was finished," Cardinal Rossi intoned. "He had to stay at the altar until it was complete. Like all of us, he stayed with the cross until his life came to a close. I know he offered himself to our Blessed Lord, praying unceasingly, worshipping faithfully, knowing that when his life had run its course, he would be in the divine embrace. So death is not the end. So death is not the conclusion. If you seek the salvation and redemption of God, like the monsignor, death allows you to soar into the sweetness of life with our Blessed Father. The way Monsignor Ryan lived in this life determined the way he will spend eternity."

As the local and national politicians who were present leaned forward to hear him talk from the soul, the cardinal moved from behind the podium. He kept his voice low, mellow, and full of bass tones.

"Monsignor Ryan realized he had to go back to his Father's house and the blessedness of heaven," said the fat, squat man in the flowing red robes. "He realized the truth in, and the value of, the sacraments. He realized the integrity of the Last Word and the Last Gospel from the apostles, which says that the Father molds the history and rhythms of the life of a man and a woman. He realized we all must go back to the beginning of all beginnings."

The cardinal coughed and wiped his face. "Monsignor Ryan understood the moment of consecration," he noted. "He knew the significance of the blood and the body, as well as the importance of the Calvary and the Crucifixion. He knew the duty and responsibility of the faithful, living up to the sacred call of our Blessed Lord. 'This is my body. This is my blood.' He knew that we, as the faithful, are called to suffer with Christ so that we can reign with Him."

He let out a soft sob. "Monsignor Ryan was a great example to the faithful. He redeemed himself in union with our Blessed Lord. He applied His merits to his soul by being like Him in all things. Thank you, Monsignor Ryan. Bless you as you go through the gates of paradise. Rest in peace."

Pulling me aside, one of the church staff whispered to me that the body of the monsignor had been shipped back from Sudan minus his hands and his tongue. One of the militias dumped the corpse, like a sack of rotten potatoes, near one of the refugee camps. Aid workers discovered the body and arranged to ship it back to America.No one in the congregation knew this fact, and I was warned not to tell anyone.

Some people left before the funeral service ended. I was one of them, as it dragged on and on. I had paid my respects and had grown tired of all the dignitaries, both religious and political, getting their chance at the mike. Some of these folks hadn't given Monsignor Ryan the time of day. A few of them had ignored his requests for help with the parish when it was in dire straits.

As I made my way toward the doors, I came to a stop before a large statue of the martyred Christ, His tormented head encircled by a crown of thorns, His outstretched hands marred by the nails driven into His palms on the cross. I was struck by how lifelike the figure was, down to the splatters of blood on His twisted legs.

Suddenly, I felt a tug on my sleeve. I turned, somewhat startled by the interruption. I had been so deep in thought, imagining what agony the Lord must have felt when the Roman soldiers pounded the metal spikes into the tender flesh of His palms.

"Well, the church gave Ryan a good send-off, don't you think?" said a balding white man with a slight humpback.

"He deserved it and more," I replied.

"My name is Dr. Bentley Gomes, and I know who you are," he said gruffly. "Ryan talked about you all the time. He thought a lot of you."

"That's good of him," I said. "He was a good man. Where did you know him from?"

As we talked, we walked through the church, then pushed our way through the crowd gathered at the doors. He shook a few hands on our way out. I was curious, as everybody seemed to know him.

"I knew him from his work in Africa, from Rwanda to Darfur to the Congo," he said as we started down the steps. "There is an abundance of wicked deeds being done in Africa. Ryan was determined to bring people there consolation and salvation, but the wretched continent has its share of scoundrels, maniacs, and killers with a permanent grudge against the church and those who do good."

"Maybe that's where he was when he dropped out of sight," I said.

"Ryan was moving around all over the place," Gomes said. "We had many talks about why the faith community in America should get involved in Africa, which he called 'a mission of purity and integrity, despite all the challenges or obstacles.' He was truly a servant of good."

"That sounds like him." I chuckled.

"How well did you know him?"

We reached the street and looked for a cab in the rushing traffic. A homeless woman, smelling very foul, stuck out her soiled hand for money. Gomes ignored her. I took a wad of bills out of my pants pocket and peeled off a couple of dollars. I stretched out my hand, and she took the money. Without thanking me, the woman drifted off and walked up to another person, holding out her hand.

"I hate beggars and the like," Gomes said, waving his hand. "This town used to be classy without all these people underfoot. Everybody's always got their hand out, asking for something for nothing."

I frowned. "These are hard times. Everybody's out of work."

Gomes put his hand on my shoulder and looked me dead in the eye. "This is America. If somebody wants to find a job, they can find a job. It's not like some under-privileged country, like many of the countries in Africa, where there are no opportunities. What I liked about

Ryan is that he never felt sorry for these people or catered to their weaknesses or flaws."

"The monsignor had a big heart," I replied, ignoring the obvious slur. "He was very tolerant and nonjudgmental. He looked on everybody as all God's creatures. That's why he preached the Gospel to the poor and the oppressed. He practiced what he preached."

The white man grinned. "I forgot you're a man of faith like him."

"And what does that mean?" I asked.

"You know, Christian evangelism, the conversion of sinners, and the theology of the Burning Hearts. Like Ryan, I guess you're a spiritual warrior who was chosen to save the pagans and barbarians with the Holy Word from myth and magic. Isn't that correct?"

It was my turn to grin. "You sound like a lame Jimmy Kimmel. There's a saying known to the Salvation Army, 'We are saved to serve.' I feel that is why I was baptized into the work of the Lord. To serve."

"Don't get all serious on me," Gomes said. "Ryan was like that too. All I had to do was mention the Gospel and he got defensive on me."

He reached into his pocket and produced a card with all his contact information. I looked at it. A second later a cab pulled up, and he ran to it, shouting that there would be a gathering at his place on Beekman Place next Friday and I should be there. After he climbed in the backseat, I watched the cab veer into the flow of traffic and disappear.

3

LOOK THE OTHER WAY

Lying on the sofa in the living room of my apartment the following Thursday, with a bottle of chilled Coke in her hand, Addie was more talkative than usual. She was settling in just fine. While I didn't talk much as I unloaded groceries on the kitchen table and thought about the monsignor's funeral mass, she held court, saying she was afraid to be shut up in a closed space, afraid of the time just before the dawn broke, afraid of caterpillars and snails, afraid of losing her temper, afraid of failing, and afraid of death.

"I think everybody's afraid of death," I replied, stacking the cans. "If I meet someone who says that he's not, I think he's lying, unless he's crazy. I think every person has fears and phobias, but some people let them cripple them."

"I used to live in fear," she said, shaking up the bottle and letting the soda fizz to the top. "I was very scared of my late husband. He could get violent at the drop of a hat. You never knew what would set him off."

"You said he hit you, right?" I sometimes wondered if she would ever get over her failed marriage. But I couldn't talk. We were both struggling with the ghosts of our pasts.

She allowed the soda bubbles to overflow and spill down the bottle. "Often after a hard shift at the rig, he'd blow his top. He'd take me out so the men could see me, and then he'd snipe at me all the way through dinner. He could be very mean and cruel. He could be very sarcastic and defensive if I said something that got beneath his skin."

"Did he ever say he was sorry, Addie?"

"Yes, he did." She smiled shyly, putting her thumb into the bottle.

I moved around the kitchen, carrying a bunch of cans and stacking them in the cabinet. Her expression let me know that there hadn't always been pain and torment in that relationship. Probably the making-up process, when he held her in his arms, had been delightful.

Her breathing changed, and her eyes went wide. "It was always about his life and what he wanted to do. Never about mine. His was a love that kept you from doing something you wanted to try. It held you in place. I was afraid to take risks. I was scared to make a change in my actions and thinking. He was poison to me."

I found a seat in the living room and sat staring at her. "If he had not been killed in the accident, do you think you would have left?"

"No. I was too much in love with him."

"What did you feel when they said he was dead?" I knew what she was going to say before she said it.

"I was glad he was dead," she said without the usual Southern accent in her voice. "I stopped worrying if he was finally going to love me. I knew I couldn't save him from himself. Heck, I was worried about saving myself."

My Christian heritage prevented me from wrapping her in my arms and consoling her. I was a minister, and I was a man. It was so hard to act like a heathen, to do what the world expected of black men, knowing that if I believed in the scriptures and then did the opposite, I would be deliberately choosing the wrong path.

"He set me back big-time," she said, wiping a tear or two away. "He thought I was a loser. I knew I was not. Also, I realized that those who start behind usually stay behind, and I was not going to have that."

"Why didn't you just leave?"

"I don't know. I don't know." Her hands covered her face.

"Do you think all men are like he was?" I asked her.

She dodged the issue and kept saying that pride and confidence were the bedrock of self-development and accomplishment. Her stare remained on the soda pop bottle. I wondered how long we were going to walk down torturous memory lane.

"I needed his lies," she said in a fog, her look out of focus. "I needed them to keep going. I had an odd sense of loyalty to him. I never stepped out on him."

"Did he cheat on you?" I saw her wince from the question.

Pausing before answering, she started pushing the bottle between her hands. Then she looked up and said, "Now and then . . . yeah, now and then."

Her words formed images in my mind that I found distasteful, lusty, and sinful when she described the sexual heat between them when they had a series of fights. They'd come together at night, and they'd fight and fuss during the day. The battles became so bad that they took to sleeping in separate rooms, and so he started staying out late, getting drunk. He'd come home with lipstick on his underwear, smelling of some rank female.

Her long, tapered fingers went over her watery eyes. "He kept calling, calling, calling, calling me on that last day of his life. Said he wanted us to be on good terms, said he wanted us to make up, to put our marriage back together. He said he'd be good."

"Addie, do you regret not taking him up on his offer?"

"No." She took a sip from the bottle.

"Why not?"

"Love can be very sweet, but it's too difficult and painful," she mused. "This I do know. I don't want to mess up my personal life. I can't keep starting over. Emotions can get in the way. I don't want to overthink my life."

I cleared my throat. "All I want to know is, where do I stand?"

Arriving here in Harlem meant she'd earned her moment of grace. No longer would she have to be trampled underfoot by horny farmhands and oil-rig workers, and new doors were opening. She didn't want to miss those opportunities.

"I think we both need some time," she replied.

"Addie, I don't think you can speak for both of us," I said, my voice strong and quiet. I knew I needed her. I'd needed her for a long time, because I was tired of suffering with dignity. No man was above the laws of nature. We all needed to have love and affection in our lives, although there were many of us who prided ourselves on our self-control and self-discipline. To be truthful, life was passing us by.

"Bet you'll drop me like a hot potato for one of those slick, sophisticated city gals," she said, pulling her head back. "I'll always appreciate that you let me escape with you from down there. Still, you'll want one of those city gals, fashionably skinny, all bones. What do they call it? Anorexic?"

"That's what they call it," I said, grinning.

She sighed dramatically. "Besides, I don't know what love looks like or feels like anymore. Why don't we take it slow?"

"Okay. You're calling the shots."

Addie stood up, shaking off the last round of our dialogue, and began talking about her new girlfriend from the hair salon. Her description of Jewel, the buxom hairdresser, was really wild. She could really read people, especially women and city dwellers.

"My friend is pretty aggressive and loud." She chuckled. "She likes to yell and scream in order to get things done. She thinks she's really sexy . . . a bombshell. I don't like how she tears people down to make herself look good. Everybody knows how insulting she can be."

"How can you be pals with somebody like that?"

"It's all right," she replied. "When I want to make a point, I interrupt her and talk over her. She doesn't like it one bit. She tells me I'm snooty and competitive, but all she wants is to control me."

"Now, what does she do again?" My question permitted me to catch my breath. She didn't seem like the kind of woman Addie would befriend.

After she told me about their tour of Sugar Hill and the site of the Audubon Ballroom, where Malcolm X was gunned down, she further explained the mystique of the enigmatic hairdresser.

"Jewel's what they call 'a beauty professional.' She knows heaps about cosmetics, make-up, and stuff like blush," she said. "She is an expert on rouge, wrinkle creams, and stuff to conceal dark circles under the eyes."

"My aunt used to be a hairdresser. Did women in her living room," I remarked. "I remember the smell of burnt hair and the shrieks when she scorched their ears with the hot comb. Boy, those ladies could gossip."

I really didn't know Addie. I liked her. Still, I wondered if she was calculating and ruthless, like some of the women I'd met in the city, or if maybe she was just putting on an act. Good, straightforward country gal. This mask suited her just fine.

"How is your Harlem tour going, Addie?"

She didn't respond at first. "I found out Harlem is controlled by outside forces. Very little of it is black-owned anymore. And the neighborhood is changing from the place I read about to something else. Jewel had a lot to say about that. It's more white than I thought it was."

"A lot of the black neighborhoods are changing like that . . . becoming gentrified, with more whites coming in."

At least Addie and I talked about everything and nothing. I liked that. Sometimes Terry had been silent for days, weeks. It had been unnerving. Showing that she didn't miss a trick, Addie asked me about all the packs of chewing gum around the apartment. She was like a detective from one of those film noirs, a bronze Dick Tracy.

"Do you have a thing with your mouth?" she quizzed me. "I think they call it an oral fixation. I bet you used to smoke."

I cleared my throat. "You guessed it. I did smoke, for a long time. I loved to smoke after meals or after church, just to unwind. Smoking got me through some tough times. I couldn't relax without it, without a cigarette."

"My husband smoked reefers. Said it put his mind at ease," she said.

"None of that for me. I've got enough problems without that."

"Clint, when did you quit smoking cigarettes? I never see you smoke, unless you're doing it on the sly."

"I quit for good after my wife killed herself. I figured it wasn't doing me any good. I still crave it sometimes."

She laughed wickedly. "I never smoked. One doctor I saw on the television said there is a link between thumb sucking and smoking cigarettes. I bet he's right."

"I wouldn't know about that," I said quietly.

She breathed deeply, keeping some distance between us. It was almost as if she thought I could contaminate her just by touching her.

I looked puzzled. "Thanks for being in my life. You've given me a ray of hope for normalcy. I'll be a human being again. I won't forget it."

She walked into the kitchen and got another bottle of Coke from the icebox. Soda pop was her weakness. "I won't let you forget it."

"By the way, we're going to dinner tomorrow night," I said. "I think you'll like it. These are folks you'll really enjoy. Are you free tomorrow night?"

She closed her eyes, relishing the fact that she was here, in New York City. These were the things—the incredible events, the memorable situations—that made this place so attractive and interesting. A nod of her pretty head told me all that I wanted to know. It would be an evening that would change our lives forever.

4

ROCK MY SPIRIT

Everything had been previously arranged for the special night. We were in fancy dress, formal attire. I loved how she looked in that designer dress, a knockoff that she bought for the occasion at Macy's. They sent a car to take us to the dinner, which was for some Congolese refugees and was being held downtown, at the home of one of Dr. Gomes's friends. It was switched at the last moment by an organizer. The event turned out to be actually a fundraiser for Operation Salvation.

When we arrived, a uniformed gentleman escorted us upstairs to the event. Outside a closed door, another staffer waved at us to stop, then peeked inside the room. Finally, he motioned us inside the room and indicated that we should sit along the back wall. As we made our way to the only empty seats there, a documentary played on a screen, and we were bombarded with horrible images: a young woman mourning her dead infant; two foreign doctors tending to a teenager who was suffering from malaria; a malnourished older man, with a skeletal frame, sitting on a bench; a group of frightened refugees holding out their hands for food that was being distributed by UN members; and a row of corpses laying alongside a dirt road.

"This is crazy, totally crazy . . . black people killing other black people," Addie whispered before some man asked her to be quiet.

The lights came on, and we could see that there were about twenty people seated around a long oak table, with food and drink before them. They were dressed formally as well. All the people around the table were white, affluent, with a touch of sophistication about them. I noticed five people sitting along the wall in the front. They were blacks and were dressed cleanly, and yet they had a ravaged appearance. They were the focus of all the attention. The room itself was very grand and elegant, like a venue you'd find in a four-star hotel.

"In the heart of Africa, there is a war for the soul of the continent," said a man who introduced himself as Owen Yemma. "The nearly two decades of war in the Congo have been bloody and horrific. A group of Congolese rebels, known as M twenty-three, has routed the national army in the eastern sectors of the country, displacing civilians, who pour into a small number of camps in Rwanda—"

A woman, her blond hair piled on top of her head, screwed up her horse face and interrupted the speaker. "Tell them, Owen. Tell them how Rwanda has welcomed these displaced civilians with militias affiliated with the rebels, and how these proxies have killed thousands of innocent people. Rwanda denies that fact. Tell them, Owen."

Owen took a drink of his water and continued. "That's true. Rwanda has flip-flopped on its responsibility to the refugees. The media and UN observers see war at its most brutal. They have witnessed rape being used against Congolese girls and women. Anything goes as far as the militias and the national army are concerned. They do whatever they want, without any worry of arrest and punishment. The UN peacekeepers have been ineffective in stopping these atrocities."

"Are both sides guilty of using child soldiers in the Congo?" a man asked. I saw how some of the other guests were looking at the refugees, who appeared uneasy and fidgety.

"I know the International Criminal Court at The Hague has prosecuted many of the major perpetrators of this crime against children, including one of the rebel commanders, Thomas Lubanga," Owen replied. "He was sentenced to fourteen years in prison for his use of child soldiers. Progress is being made, but it's not enough so far. The rebels are being subsidized by other nations. I recall Rwanda and Uganda attacked the Congo to rout the people responsible for the previous atrocities. Some in the Western world have said that the rest of the African countries did very little to keep the peace or to stop the carnage."

Two of the whites, both of them impeccably dressed and with deep pockets, interrupted Owen as he continued his history lesson on the Congo. One of them shouted, "What about the child soldiers? Are they still being used in the violence in the region?"

Refusing to be deterred, Owen waved them off. "The West believes there are no easy solutions for the African crisis. They can't explain the failings and defects of the sub-Saharan continent. It seems that the new leaders transform themselves into dictators and despots and are concerned only with their greed and excess."

Another moneyman put his hand underneath his long chin and said with a frown, "So why should we get involved? Why should we invest in a losing cause?"

Owen pointed his finger accusingly at the man. "Because we cannot afford to sit on the sidelines and let this tragedy continue. Also, we know the causes. Most Africans in the region blame outsiders for their troubles and say that if these agitators would leave, then everything would return to normal."

"And what is *normal?*" another do-gooder said, laughing. Some of the others snickered under their breath, but the people devoted to the campaign screwed up their faces.

I looked at Addie, who shrugged at the insensitivity of those who had pledged their energy to the African crisis. We whispered to each other that this was probably how most people in the West saw every human crisis over in Africa. If this crisis had erupted anyplace in Europe or Asia or Latin America, relief and supplies would have been airlifted to the area.

Owen was undaunted in his mission of good will. "We're not there to solve the political questions. We're there to meet their basic health needs. You're mistaken if you think that we're the UN, that we have a cure for the rampant corruption or the ethnic hatred engulfing the region. We're trying to do the Lord's will. We're trying to reach out to those who need our help and support."

The image of a relief worker, a healthy young white woman, carrying a starving boy with a ravaged face and a bloated stomach appeared on the screen. Flies settled in the child's nostrils and mouth. The people gathered around the table stopped talking, while others in the room covered their eyes. It was a pitiful sight.

"Charity or philanthropy?" Owen asked.

The white faces turned to the speaker, who continued talking as images of malnourished children and women, of corpses lined up beside refugee tents, of staffers trying to force liquids down parched throats, and of villagers without limbs, reprisals by the rebels, flashed on the screen.

"The Congo is a mess," Owen said angrily. "It has been a mess for a long time. This is the region where the Mobutu dictatorship reigned for over three decades and was violently overthrown only in nineteen ninety-seven.

Then Mobutu was followed by another despot, Laurent Kabila, and now there are unceasing waves of killing and bloodshed throughout the land."

A black woman dressed severely in black, with a large gold cross around her neck, stood up and asked one of the most important questions of the meeting. "Why must Americans always have to come to the rescue? We've got enough to do on our shores. There's all kinds of misery and need here. Africans need to stand up and take responsibility for their own actions—"

Addie interrupted her. "That could be said about American blacks. Maybe if we stood up and redirected our energy in our communities, we'd end the misery here."

The woman jerked her face toward Addie. "And who are you? Who invited you to this private meeting?"

"I'm a guest of Dr. Gomes, who is a friend of Mr. Yemma there," she replied. "Just call me Addie. I don't like your snooty tone, ma'am. I thought this was a Christian organization."

"We're all good Christians here," the woman retorted.

Owen put a finger to his lips, trying to nip the brewing dispute in the bud. "Whether it's volunteerism or grassroots goodwill, this is not about Rudyard Kipling's 'white man's burden.' We're trying to keep people alive, trying to give them peace and comfort. This is why we're meeting all this week with a number of charitable foundations and individual donors. We need medical supplies, doctors and nurses, and essentials like water, food, clothing, and tents. We cannot turn our backs on these underserved areas."

Another color image of lifeless bodies covered with blankets in a large tent appeared on the screen behind Owen as he turned the audience's attention to the quintet of Africans in the room, who looked around at the prosperous men and women in their midst.

"Look at these poor souls," Owen said mournfully. "There are all kinds of evil going on over there. Murders, numerous cases of child and woman rape, plunder, displacement. When it's time, the plague of flagrant human rights abuses will need to be addressed, but that is not our job."

A black-and-white image of dark-skinned skeletons, arranged in order of age and height and propped up against a mud wall, to be fed by a group of relief workers, appeared on the screen. Some of the weaker ones slid down to the ground.

"Have you ever seen a human being in such a malnourished condition?" Owen asked them. "Starving to death?"

Annoyed, the black woman with the large gold cross muttered under her breath, folding her arms. One or two of her cronies rolled their eyes, because they thought Owen was laying it on too thick.

"Extreme hunger sets in, and the body starts to die. It begins to eat itself in order to live," Owen said slowly for effect. "When hunger totally takes over, all thoughts, all movements cease. And the person slumps to the ground and waits to hear his or her last breath."

Owen paused, looking around the room to see if his words were hitting home. His relief organization needed funds, and if he had to plead and grovel, then so be it.

"The suffering is so great for these refugees in the Congo," he began again. "They think they have been targeted and singled out by an unconcerned God. A white God who has turned His back on them. You know how Americans hate anything that entails suffering and its aftermath. They like happy endings, like everything tied up neatly with a bow."

Looking around the room, I thought that these people were not the kind of audience that Owen should expect to be generous. These were the kind of folks who sought tax loopholes, offshore accounts, and financial sure shots.

"Stand up, Kwesi," Owen said quietly.

A Congolese boy, probably in his teens, stood, his suit dwarfing his slight frame. His gaze was toward the floor. He was embarrassed to be the center of attention.

"Tell them what happened to you," Owen said.

"The rebels killed my mother and father and made me shoot my grandfather," the boy mumbled, his dark purple face glistening. "I saw them rape my sister and my aunt, many of them. They made me fight with them."

"Were you a child soldier?" a white man quizzed him.

"Yes," the boy said, his eyes lowered. "I ran away during battle, when they were not looking. They found me."

"Did you hate fighting for the devils who killed your family?" another man asked, adjusting his lapel. "How did that make you feel?"

Wounded to the heart, the boy sat down, staring blankly ahead, wringing his bony hands.

"What kind of questions are those?" Owen chided.

"I'm very sorry," the man said, apologizing.

Owen lifted his hand and asked one of the girls to stand. "Kenia, what happened to you? Tell them your story."

The girl, with a horrible machete wound along her cheek, stood trembling, her eyes bright and focused on Owen. She was dressed casually in a white blouse and a golden cotton dress that reached down to her knobby knees. Everyone waited for her to find her words.

When a murmur arose in the room, suddenly she sat back down, smoothed her dress, and stared straight ahead. Tears ran down her cheeks. I felt Addie shudder against me. She was scowling at the lack of compassion shown by some of those gathered there.

"Yes, Congolese people know what suffering is," Owen noted after explaining that the girl had been sexually assaulted and left for dead. She could not bring herself to discuss the atrocities she had endured.

He paused for a moment and then pleaded once again with the group. "America cannot turn its back on them when they need us the most. They need our help, not our pity. One can either act or shut one's eyes and pretend this misery does not exist. I see another one of our visitors, who was invited at the request of our good friend Dr. Gomes. The doctor has been a hardworking, loyal supporter of this organization and its work. Do you care to stand and give us your opinion of our effort?"

Addie nudged me on the shoulder. "He means you."

I put on a brave face and rose to my full length. "As the apostle Matthew said, 'Freely ye have received, freely give.' Sometimes it's our mandate not just to minister to those around us, but also to practice that ministry in the neediest places of the world. As Christians, we must see that those things that are out of balance in God's Kingdom are set right. As Christians, our ministry says we must show compassion and appeal to our conscience when we come to know Christ. That ministry demands action and hard work sometimes. I commend each and every one of you for the fine and courageous work your organization is doing in Africa. May God bless your work."

Addie smiled at me. "Not bad. Not bad for words off the cuff."

While the group applauded me politely, Owen wrapped up the meeting, thanking the members and guests for their time. Addie couldn't get out of there quick enough. We didn't stay for the meal. Once we were outside, she complained that certain members were hypocrites, that they were not really concerned about the charitable work the organization was doing or about the African people.

In the cab back uptown, Addie talked about how she wanted to see one of her old friends, Lester "The Human Mule" Moore, who was making an appearance soon over in Harlem's Marcus Garvey Park. Lester, she told me, was from Anniston and was a pal of her mama's from the old days. The old geezer, in his late eighties, was going to pull a small van with his teeth and a chain over in the park. I declined to go with her.

But the other bombshell she dropped on me was that she planned to go to Sudan, which, according to the UN, was facing the worst humanitarian crisis in the world at that moment. She explained that she wanted to do some good over there, that we needed more time to make a commitment to each other, and that she didn't want to lose any days as she waited for me to make up my mind whether I wanted her or not.

5

INTO THE FIRE

This was the first time I'd ever heard Addie mention Sudan or Darfur. I wondered how she first came to the conclusion that she needed to be in that accursed place. Everything was the Congo this, the Congo that. But she decided Sudan was the place to go. I went on the computer and researched Sudan, and what I read stunned me with fear. Sudan, the largest African country, had a bloody history of conflict and had been immersed in a violent civil war for over two decades. Since its independence from Britain in 1956, there had been bloodshed since 1983, with the northern Sudanese, largely Arab and Muslim tribes, clashing with the southern Sudanese, who were mostly Christian. I was shocked that this recent civil war had cost more than two million deaths, despite a supposed truce signed by Sudan and South Sudan a short time ago. Although I continued to research the crisis in Sudan, there was so much I did not know.

"Why would you want to go to Sudan when wholesale killing is going on there?" I asked Addie while we were walking two days after the meeting through Marcus Garvey Park in Harlem.

"Why?" She turned and made a face. "I want to go because there's suffering there. I think I can make a difference."

I came to a halt and just stood there, looking at her incredulously. "There's suffering here. There's suffering here in Harlem. Why can't you make a difference here in the States?"

She put her hands on her hips, taking a defiant stance. "I saw your notes on the kitchen table. If you read all the Google entries about Sudan, then you read that the Sudanese have no money, no schools, no hospitals, nothing. Also, the war has driven more than four million people from their land. I've got to help out in some way."

"What can you do?" I asked when we finally resumed our walk.

"Clint, I know this sounds crazy, but I must go there." She grinned. "I can't ask you to come along,because you have your life to live here. Let me go. I might learn something."

"Who has been filling your head with this tripe?" I asked.

"Mr. Gomes has been talking to me since the meeting about how it's so important to volunteer our services there since they have so little," she replied, reaching the curb. "He said he will make all the arrangements for me to get there. He knew I would go. The need there is so great."

However, that was not the end of it. The following week, Addie did her best to avoid me, until I caught her leaving her place one morning. I rushed up to her, grabbed her by the elbow. She gave me a nasty look.

"Why have you been avoiding me?" I asked.

"I've been busy," she answered. "I've got so much to do."

Having cornered her, I made the most of it. "This is not a cruise. This trip to Sudan is life and death, complete with bombings, kidnappings, hijackings, and shootings. Do you really know what you are going into?"

"Yes, I do," she said, nodding. I noticed lines in her brown face that I hadn't noticed before. She was dressed in jogging clothes, so I guessed I'd interrupted her morning run.

"I talked to Gomes as well," I mentioned.

"What did he say, Clint?"

"Gomes said Sudan is heating up, with all kinds of acts of terrorism," I said while crossing the street. "He also said there are extremists who are kidnapping senior government officials, expatriates, foreign travelers, and demanding ransoms. There have been kidnappings of peacekeepers and volunteers in Darfur and in areas near Chad and the Central African Republic. Sudan is a most dangerous place."

She put her hands up and trotted off down the street. Her mind was made up. She had decided to make the trip, and that was that. I stood there for a moment and simply watched her as she put distance between us, then turned and headed home.

Upon my return to my apartment, I settled in front of my computer and consulted a list of local laws and customs for Sudan, noting that the country's dominant authority was Muslim. A Web site geared to foreign travelers said that they should respect all local traditions, customs, laws, and, most of all, religions. In Sudan, the tenets of the holy month of Ramadan had to be respected, and since the chief law practiced was sharia law, that meant no alcohol, no carousing with a woman other than your wife—meaning no females could be invited into your hotel room—and no homosexual acts, ever. The law stipulated that a non-Muslim woman didn't have to wear a veil or cover her head, but she could never dress in a wanton manner. I took this to mean that short skirts, tight pants, and breasts spilling out of a seductive blouse were forbidden.

What did Addie think she would do in a restrictive situation like this? How was she going to help? Even if she followed every rule, every law, she could still get into trouble with the moral police, Sudan's National Intelligence and Security Service. They had plenty of plainclothes agents everywhere, waiting, watching for one false step.

The Web site provided a list of recommended vaccinations for foreign travelers and noted that the health-care facilities in Khartoum, Sudan's capital, were fair, but the hospitals were not prepared to handle serious medical problems. It advised anyone traveling to the country to get adequate travel health insurance and have enough money on hand to cover the costs of any medical treatment, evacuation, and a flight home.

I reached for my phone and dialed a former relief worker I knew, a friend of Dr. Smart. He provided me with a phone number for emergency medical assistance at Fedail Hospital in Khartoum: 083 741 426 (press #241 for English). He also advised me to avoid eating contaminated food and to drink water that was safe. And he warned me not to share bodily fluids, and cautioned me to reduce my exposure to germs and to know where to get effective medical care while traveling. Before hanging up, he said, "Travel safe and be aware of your surroundings."

Yes, I was going. I was going to be with her. I loved her. I wanted to keep her safe. I wanted to watch over her.

I devoted the next few days to learning everything I needed to do before embarking on this journey. Some people who worked for the International Red Cross advised me to work out my travel arrangements, get my documents current, and make sure my visa was up to date in case I had to leave quickly. The people at the British Embassy could assist me in a time of crisis, but their response might be very limited. I wondered about the status of our embassy over there.

Sudan was not a pleasing tribute to the liberation movements of such leaders as Kwame Nkrumah and Jomo Kenyatta. It was not a prime example of Africa for Africans. And what was I, a Christian minister, going to do there? With a message of love and hope, some ministers, conscious of their global obligations, talked about the notion of church building in the poorest lands. Through Him, Jesus Christ, I'd learn to understand suffering, not like what I saw in Harlem or in the Deep South, but in the violence of Sudan by spreading the Gospel like water on the embers of misery.

Watching high-powered ministers on TV sell themselves from their mega-churches, I realized that we in the church were more concerned with ministering to the saved and the membership than with showing compassion or acceptance to the lost and the broken. We stepped over the poor and the needy. We didn't look on mercy as a blessed gift. We didn't realize that mercy required hard work. We didn't know the fruits of mercy were hard earned. I remembered the framed quotation from Mother Teresa on the wall of Dr. Smart's office: "We think sometimes that poverty is only being hungry, naked, and homeless. The poverty of being unwanted, unloved, and uncared for is the greatest poverty."

Once I had an idea of what the trip entailed, I called Addie one evening and notified her that I was coming with her. She laughed and said she had figured I would do that.

"You can't let me out of your sight for one moment, huh?" she joked, and then she asked if I had begun preparing for the Sudan trip.

"There's so much to do." My voice betrayed the fatigue that had come with trying to nail down all the requirements of this journey over the past few days. I was almost completely worn out.

She coughed harshly. "Don't bring one of those disposable cameras. The authorities don't like cameras or anyone taking pictures in Sudan. You can't take pictures near government buildings, military bases, bridges, or airports. They're very nervous about that kind of thing."

"Think about the chaos of that place," I said. "Maybe we need to reconsider this trip. If we break any of their rules , they can throw us out for visa irregularities or impose severe penalties, such as imprisonment. Or we could get shot."

Her laugh echoed through the phone. "You're not going to punk out on me. I thought you were going to go with me so you could protect me from myself. You sound like a fraidy cat. After all we went through during our last adventure, during our Mason-Dixon journey, this should be as easy as cherry pie. Promise me that you'll come."

"You have my word," I replied, a chill going up my spine. I heard her laugh real nasty before I hung up the phone.

6

RETHINKING MALICE

The flight to Khartoum took over fourteen hours because of bad weather, equipment failure, the loss of luggage, and civil disobedience. Addie loved all of it, while I went nuts over these glitches in our trip. Under the blazing African sun, the airport was bustling. People were walking everywhere, guarded by an unit of government soldiers carrying sidearms, Through the windows I saw vans loaded with tourists stopped at checkpoints that led to a slew of airlines, such as Emirates, Badr Airlines, EgyptAir, Kenya Airways, Etihad Airways, Saudia, Royal Jordanian Airlines, and Sudan Airways. I could feel eyes on me.

A greeting committee met us inside the airport, with lots of laughter and promises of good food and restful hours before we headed south. I talked to a representative of the Sudanese government, who assured us of safe passage anywhere and said he would provide us with security when we drove to our hotel.

A man, a regal-looking gent dressed in a sleek white Italian suit, tugged at my sleeve outside of the air terminal. He introduced himself as an editor of the Sudanese newspaper *Al-Tayar*, which was published in the nation's capital. He wondered if I could find time for him before I went on a tour of the refugee camps. I was very curious about what he had to say. Two men in civilian clothes and shades lurked nearby as we spoke.

"I might have trouble with this heat," I said, wiping my forehead.

The editor laughed. "This is nothing. Wait until you go south."

"Let's go to the hotel," Addie said, smiling, when our car pulled up to the curb. "I feel so grimy and sweaty. The sun is just beating down on me so strongly."

I pivoted to the editor, having forgotten his name that quickly, and told him that I'd meet with him after we got settled at the hotel. The staff put our things in the rear of a new white Land Rover, slammed the doors after we climbed in, and off we went to the modest three-story hotel that would serve as our temporary residence.

We checked in quickly, and then I walked Addie to her room.

"I'll talk to you as soon as I wash up," Addie said, then disappeared into her room. That was the last I saw of her that day.

I found my room and placed my luggage on the table next to my bed. Then I sat down on a chair and put my head on top of my suitcase. Sweat had soaked my shirt and pants. Yes, there was a rickety fan, which was battling to keep a decent breeze blowing in the small room. I looked around and saw a tiny refrigerator, a telephone, a portable TV, and a short stack of local magazines. With great effort, I pulled myself up and went to the window, which looked out on a busy side street.

It was like a *National Geographic* photograph, rich with dark people in colorful clothing, who were going every which way, carrying fruit or crates. I had noticed on the way here that there were jeeps stationed all throughout the city, filled with heavily armed soldiers. Owen had warned me that undercover agents of the police also monitored the civilians, as well as the tourists.

The telephone rang. It was Addie.

"It's wonderful!" she exclaimed. "Just like I imagined it."

I was less impressed. "I guess."

She wasn't going to let me dampen her enthusiasm. "Well, I could be in a New York City schoolroom with a bunch of snotty kids. Delores, one of the teachers I know in the city, told me how the kids all think they are special. They don't think they have to study or act civilly in the classroom. You, as a teacher, have to play parent or cop. You can't yell at them. You can't discipline them. I didn't think I was ready for that."

"Was that a part of your decision to come here?" I asked.

"Yes, a part of it." Her voice quivered.

"Can't you work at a charter school? That would be better than a public school. I hear some of the public schools are pretty crummy."

She sniffed. "Charters are no better than the public schools. That's what national studies show. And what edge they have has to do with the fact that they accept fewer special education students and foreign students who have to learn English as a second language."

"If you feel this way, then maybe it was best that you didn't try to get hired as a public school teacher," I replied. "Also, I guess it's a big adjustment, going from a small rural school to a big city public school. The requirements are totally different."

I could hear her swallow in frustration. "No, I disagree. The goal of teaching is to prepare the kids for life, to give them the proper skills to hit the ground running. Delores says these kids in the public schools are so sure of themselves, so confident, but when they are compared to kids around the world, especially Asians, they come up short academically. They lag behind. They don't know everything you need to know to compete in this high-tech world."

Pulling the chair over to where I stood by the window, I straddled it. "So what are you going to do after our Sudan adventure? Have you thought about that?"

"I don't know, Clint," she said softly.

"Well, that's fair enough," I answered. "Who knows what will happen here. I hope we don't have a repeat of our Dixie journey. My goal is to get through this in one piece."

I heard her crumpling up newspaper or something, and then she spoke quietly. "We will. Well, I'm worn out. Serious jet lag. I'm going to get some sleep. What are you going to do?"

I wished I had a cigarette. "I'm supposed to meet a man about our trip to the refugee camps. He's going to give me the lowdown on this place, the dos and don'ts, so we don't take a wrong step."

"Okay, Well, I'm too tired to talk anymore. I'll see you later, Clint," Addie said.

As soon as we hung up, the telephone rang again. It was the front desk, asking me if they could put through a call from the editor Addie and I had met at the airport. The man was impatient and wanted to make sure that we would have our meeting. I wondered what was so important. The government had its people planted everywhere.

The call, when we finally got through, wasn't taken by the editor himself, but by one of his aides, who alerted me that a car would come for me in half an hour. The editor was assuming I would be ready. To tell the truth, I was totally bushed, so tired that I'd probably fall asleep in the meeting. I could barely keep my eyes open.

However, I managed to shower and shave. After drinking two cups of black coffee, I was ready for action, almost alert. I dressed in my white suit and a light yellow shirt, then donned my sandals. Maybe I shouldn't have done this, but my feet were aching from the long flight, so regular shoes were out of the question.

When I went down to the street ten minutes later, accompanied by one of the editor's staff, who, I noticed, wore a gun, I saw three plainclothes guys, possibly from the government's security forces. They made no effort to conceal the fact that they were watching me closely. In fact, once the staffer and I got in the car, they followed us directly to the newspaper offices and parked at the curb, near the front of the English-designed building.

I walked behind the staffer through the halls, trying to match his quick strides. He opened the reinforced door and stood inside to let me pass. The editor, dressed in a gray business suit, met me at the door and shook my hand vigorously. Then he led me into his office. Two of his aides followed us into the room. Introductions were made. He smoked cigarettes, English cigarettes, and tried to avoid blowing the fumes in my face.

"How do you like it so far?" he asked, the tobacco stains on his teeth showing as he spoke.

I laughed, then replied, "I'll tell you in a couple of weeks."

Observing the niceties, he invited me to take a seat in a chair in front of his desk and then introduced himself again as Reik Hasseem, editor of one of the four newspapers in northern Sudan. I dropped into it and watched him. He sat down behind his desk and launched into a discussion of the current situation in Sudan. He told me that democracy would probably not take root in his country, because there are two major factors militating against it, one tribal and the other spiritual. Muslim against Christian. Then he addressed the role that the United States had played in Sudan.

"Like Clinton, Obama has no guts," Hasseem remarked nastily in heavily accented English. "In two thousand ten Obama used the annual conference at the UN to bring attention to the crisis in my country. We thought he would bring peace. We thought he would do nothing like Clinton did with Rwanda. If he had pushed for a referendum to sever the country, to recognize the Islamist government in Khartoum and the largely Christian black population in the south, the current catastrophe could have been avoided."

"I think the president was battling some enemies at home. The GOP in Congress was trying to prevent him from making any progress on his domestic agenda," I answered. "He was also trying to fix the sick American economy. The previous president has wrecked it with two wars that the United States could not afford."

"But Obama, as a black man, must have realized the importance of Africa," the editor suggested. "After all, he's part African. This was a golden opportunity for him to do something great."

"Obama had his hands full," I said, watching his two aides, who were staring at me from their posts near the door. "He was putting his fingers into too many holes in the dyke. He ran out of fingers."

Hasseem snorted. "At least Bush did something. His people got an agreement from both sides, ending the conflict between the government and the rebels. He also got assurances from us that we would allow the southerners to vote in five years on whether they would remain part of Sudan or would gain their independence." I was starting to feel like a stupid American. "Do you know your Sudanese history, Reverend?"

I sat up in my seat, my expression betraying my surprise. "How did you know I was a pastor?"

The editor waved some press clippings at me and told me that they had done their homework. "I know everything about you, what happened to your family, what happened to you at your church in Harlem, what happened to you in Alabama. If I know all this about you, you can be assured the government's security forces know more."

I was stunned. I smacked my hand against my sweaty forehead. "Oh, man, maybe that is why I was followed here."

"As a Muslim, I support the government. Not in every-thing it does, but most of its actions," he said, nodding his head at his aides. "You know about Darfur. Some terrible things have happened there, but still our president, Omar al-Bashir, must do what is necessary."

"The West doesn't like it," I countered. They especially didn't like it when the Islamic Sudanese government showed their might against Darfur's non-Arab people in 2003, launching a full-scale ethnic cleansing. The West called it genocide, which is what it was. Your president allowed it to happen."

"He doesn't care about the West and what it says," Hasseem answered. "Do you know why he doesn't, my American pastor friend?"

I shook my head. "I don't know."

" Our president still ignores the will of southern Sudan to govern itself. Also, there is oil there in the south. Some eighty percent of our country's oil reserves are there, so the war continues."

"The UN doesn't like it, none of it," I argued. "There is genocide occurring there, full-scale genocide."

He leaned back, snapped his fingers, and one of the aides sprinted from the room. I noticed then that a portrait of a smiling president Omar al-Bashir had been strategically placed on the wall behind Hasseem, right over his head, and two leather-bound Korans sat on a shelf behind him.

"Obama is weak," he said and smiled. "He tried to convince our president to end the conflict by saying that he would remove the ban on American investments in

Sudanese oil exploration. That didn't work. Obama also offered to remove Sudan from the list of states sponsoring terrorism. We rejected him outright. We don't need American charity."

I understood this cavalier attitude, because I'd read somewhere that China had been bankrolling Sudan's energy projects for some time. The Chinese really didn't care about human rights. Black Christians didn't matter when it came to potential profits. Also, several Arab moneymen had lined up to cash in. So Sudan was doing quite nicely without American investment.

"Also, America is worried about Yemen and Somalia, since they're very full of followers of Osama bin Laden," he smirked. "Like Bush, Obama is nervous about national security matters . . . about terrorism and energy. Some of his advisers believe Africa is becoming an incubator for terror. What do you think?"

"I don't know," I replied right before the aide returned with a tray containing two tall cups of chilled tea. "That's what I'm here to see. I want to see for myself before I draw any conclusions."

"That's good," he said, offering me a cup. "I'll help any way I can."

"The Western media says there is possible genocide going on in South Sudan, which the government is permitting to go on," I said boldly, watching his two aides nervously lean forward. "Do you know about that?"

"I hear things, but no decent Muslim would want to live next to a person who doesn't respect Allah," Hasseem argued. "Before we had the British controlling us, forcing us to tolerate each other. That's not the case now. South Sudan got its freedom in two thousand eleven. The fighting broke out there between the supporters of their president and those of the former vice president. They say that thousands of people have been killed and that there have been massacres. I don't know about this."

"Are you saying there is no evidence of these crimes?"

"Like you, I've seen pictures and heard supposed victims say there have been killings, but this could be trumped-up, false evidence to keep up the conflict between both sides. Do you know what I mean? The West can do many things. The CIA can do many things."

"What about the child soldiers fighting there?" I asked.

"Again, I've heard the propaganda, but this could be another trick by the West," the editor said, smiling widely. "Who knows what is true?"

"The press says schools, clinics, and health centers have been attacked," I continued. "Many women and girls have been raped, savagely and sometimes by several men. Some women and girls have been kidnapped. Children are being killed as well. What do you know about this?"

"Not much," the editor boasted. "The only thing I know is what I read in the Western press. That's why we laugh at Obama and his underling Kerry. They have no idea what this whole thing is about."

"I hope to see for myself," I said firmly.

"Reverend, I'll tell you what Kerry said during his recent tour of Africa . We had a good laugh at it," the editor said, taking a sip of the tea. "Kerry said, 'Those who are responsible for targeted killings based on ethnicity or nationality have to be brought to justice, and we are actively considering sanctions against those who commit human rights violations and obstruct humanitarian assistance.' This is a big joke. Don't you agree, Reverend?"

"I don't agree," I said strongly.

"What do you think you can do, Mr. Christian?" the Sudanese editor asked. "How can you change the situation?"

"Mr. Hasseem, I'll bring the lost and the broken a message of love and hope," I said. "I believe hate and evil can never defeat the power of love. I truly believe that. I have the mandate of Christ and His Holy Word. I must preach the Word that the Kingdom is near and that the lost and the broken can be saved."

The editor and his two aides broke into hearty laughter, so much so that the three men clutched their stomachs. I knew that my meeting was over. Still, my faith in Christ remained in me, for I knew the Lord could heal the sick, raise the dead, cleanse those who had sinned, drive out demons. I had never felt such faith and trust in the Lord and His holy scriptures as I did at that moment, there in the office of this Islamist, in the lion's den.

As the editor ushered me out of his office and through the rows of reporters hammering out their stories on computers, he ordered one of his aides to see me safely back to the hotel.

"When you return from the bush, you come and see me," he said to me on the steps outside. "Then we'll talk and see whether your opinions of our government, the opposition, Darfur, and the country have changed. I can't wait for your return."

"Yes, we'll talk. Good-bye," I said before climbing into the same car that had brought me here. The aide shut my door and then got in the front passenger seat.

Inside the car, the driver turned on the police radio, and the dispatcher announced that a bomb had ripped through one of the neighborhoods in the western part of the city. It had exploded around midday, when office workers and the privileged classes went to lunch. Witnesses said there were many casualties and fatalities amid the rubble. The aide remarked that the blast was designed to sow the seeds of fear and terror among the people of the city, who thought they were safe with the government's protection.

Following my arrival at the hotel, I went immediately to my room and dropped to my knees in earnest prayer.

What am I doing here? What can I hope to accomplish?
How can I meet the needs of the lost and the broken?
What does the Lord want me to do? Thy will is my will.

I suddenly felt dirty. . I took another shower and scrubbed the ever-present Sudanese dirt from my flesh. I scrubbed and scrubbed and scrubbed. I thought I'd never get clean. Never.

7

NAMES WITHOUT FACES

A bright and cheery Addie woke me up the next morning, pounding on my door, shouting my name. It was crazy to be so energetic at this time of the morning. She couldn't wait to get going to the refugee camps. She wanted to see everything up close, wallow in the pain and suffering of it, and find out firsthand what Sudan was all about. I could have told her. At that meeting with the editor, I got a chance to see what challenges the country faced, challenges the West could never fathom.

Yawning and stretching, I stumbled from the bed and yelled for her to give me a minute. I reached in the refrigerator for a bottle of water and drank it slowly. Wondering if my "friends" were there in front of the building, I crept to the side of the window and moved the curtain to take a peek outside. Two security members, in casual garb and shades, stood near the car, in plain sight. And one of them had binoculars directed at my window.

"Addie, one more minute," I said loudly, grabbing my robe.

When I opened the door, she walked through the doorway like a house on fire, full of energy and questions. "Where were you yesterday?"

"At the office of Mr. Hasseem, the editor. He caught me up on who the players are, what the game is, what are the stakes. I'll tell you this. Sudan is a very serious, dangerous place. After our little talk, I started wondering what we had gotten ourselves into."

"What do you mean?" she asked, prodding me for clarity.

"I know this. Christians are not welcome here," I said with dread in my voice.

"I talked to a BBC reporter last night, after I woke up," she said. "A British woman . . . very nice. She was in Rwanda during the Clinton era and said it was a slaughterhouse. She said the United States acted cowardly."

I sat on the bed and covered my legs with the blanket. "I got some of that from the editor. He thought Americans were hypocrites during the whole Rwanda thing. He said the whole world looked away from the bloodshed and the starvation, while Clinton tried to save his presidential butt. Remember Monica?"

Addie said with a dry smile, "Never again." She meant that Sudan would never meet the same fate as Rwanda when the world ignored the Rwandan genocide.

"Give me a sec so I can get washed and dressed," I said. "I'll meet you downstairs in the lobby. Is that okay?"

"Bring your camera, Clint," she said, acting like a tourist.

"No. I was warned not to bring one," I replied. "Westerners have been arrested for taking pictures around the city. The government has deemed some parts of Khartoum very sensitive, and the security officials can take you into custody for snapping pictures. This is not a town where you do a Kodak moment."

That hit Addie hard. She was just beginning to understand that Sudan was not a place where you could act like a tourist. You had to be on point. You had to get the traditions and customs right and stay well within the law.

"Wonder if I can take pictures in the refugee camps?"

"Probably, Addie. You'll have to get permission for that too."

Her expression changed, and she stiffened. "You're scaring me."

I stood up and wrapped my robe around me. "Get out of here so I can get dressed. Also, I want to pack a little bag for the trip. I don't want to leave everything to the last minute.The travel agency said they were going to reserve our rooms for us after we make our jaunt. That's good."

"That's really good," she said, beaming. "Get dressed. I want you to meet my British pal and her Egyptian friend. They're both going out to the camps with us. They know the ropes, so we won't get into trouble."

When she finally left, I checked on my two shadows on the street. Then I sat and made some notes about the meeting yesterday with the editor, which I shoved into my suitcase. In a way, I didn't want to meet Addie and her British pal. I wanted to gather my wits, so I could make this journey south.

Just then my telephone rang. It was Owen, and his voice was garbled and eventually lost in a sea of static and humming. I could have sworn someone was listening in on the other end, but it was not the time to surrender to paranoia or suspicion. The editor had tried to warn me. He had said the government kept tabs on all foreigners, especially Christians who liked to snoop, to pry into things better left alone.

In the bathroom I looked in the mirror and saw a puffy face with swollen eyelids and sighed. My hands trembled slightly as I splashed water on myself, thinking back on the talk with the Sudanese editor, concluding that I had no plan, few contacts in Sudan, and very little money. This was no joke, being here. I'd have to survive by my wits. I dried myself off with a towel and dressed hurriedly.

I left my room and moved slowly down the hallway, past a group of foreigners who were talking about the pleasures of Nairobi, the hassles of the customs officials at the airport, and the recent outbreak of the Ebola virus down south. I realized that their icy stares meant that I should not be staying at a hotel reserved for whites. What they didn't know was that I was used to this kind of treatment back in the States.

"Is your room satisfactory, sir?" an African housekeeper asked me as I passed her, and I nodded yes. Again, hateful glances came from the whites.

I searched in the lobby for any sign of Addie. The lobby was quite large, with meeting areas on the perimeter of the space, comfortable sofas for quiet moments, and seating where you could watch the activities on the street. I moved with ease through the groups of people until I saw her sitting at a table with two women, sipping coffee, a basket of French pastries between them. I approached them at a leisurely pace and came to a stop.

"How are you, Reverend Clint?" the white woman nearest to me asked, her mouth full of pastry. Her words had a British lilt mixed with an international flavor.

"Fine, ladies," I replied, bending to give Addie a smooch on her soft cheek. Honestly, I was still asleep as I stood there.

There was an empty chair at the table, and I plopped myself into it. Introductions were in order. Addie, dressed in a khaki outfit, did the honors. The woman who had initiated conversation with me was Elsa Brombert, a correspondent with the BBC. She'd been given free-floating assignments on the continent. The product of an English father and an American mother, Elsa was not attractive, but she generated a feeling of intimacy and trust upon making another's acquaintance. She possessed the rugged face of a dockhand, a long pink flamingo neck, and a sturdy body built for endurance. She loved to talk about herself. She loved the sound of her own voice.

"How long have you lived in New York?" Elsa directed the question to me.

"All my life. I'm a native New Yorker."

That triggered from her a gush of chatter about how she had attended the Columbia University Graduate School of Journalism, the J school as she called it, and had lived right around the corner from the old West End, an eatery where Jack Kerouac, the Beat legend, had supposedly hung out. She kept fooling with her brunette hair, which was tied up into a tight bun, as she spoke.

"I live not too far from there, on the other side of Morningside Park," I said, noting her pleasure that we had made a connection.

Addie said nothing, only sipped her coffee.

The other woman, an Egyptian, was very mysterious. With her model good looks, she seemed like an Arab beauty queen. In fact, she had briefly modeled for *Elle, Marie Claire,* and *Vogue.* Her wardrobe indicated that she had an adoration of Yves Saint Laurent and Diane Von Fürstenberg. It was very chic and quite out of place here.

She stared that same arrogant stare of the whites whom I'd just passed in the hallway. Perhaps, she was displaying the haughty attitude all Muslims showed practicing Christians. I learned that her name was Nawara Shobra, that she was from Cairo, and that she had gained fame when she marched alongside female protesters in her hometown's Tahrir Square in 2011.

"I don't know if you saw the famous picture of her trying to shield the young Egyptian woman who had been stripped to her bra and jeans and was being kicked and beaten by police officers," Elsa proclaimed proudly. "It ran in all the European media outlets. Did it run in the States?"

Addie didn't respond, but I replied that it probably did. However, I had paid no attention to it, since I was like most Americans, who never thought international news pertained to them. We lived in a bubble.

"The Muslim Brotherhood didn't treat them well," Elsa noted.

Giving me the fish eye, Nawara asked me a prickly question. She wanted to know if I felt at home as a black man in Africa and if Sudan had welcomed me more warmly than America. Addie started to say something, but I shot her a glance of warning. I could see who I was dealing with—a snotty, upper-class Egyptian who possibly thought all of this was beneath her.

"I'm just taking all of this in," I replied. "I'm a student. I've not drawn any conclusions or formed any opinions. I'm on a fact-finding mission."

Elsa roared with laughter, then said something about Africa being a continent of contradictions and missed opportunities, a continent addicted to tradition, tribalism, corruption, and violence. It seemed that Nawara's query had unleashed a flood of British egotism and imperial superiority. Next came Elsa's colorful résumé of her global travels.

"I was born to do this," she bragged loudly. "I've covered a malaria epidemic in Cameroon, a famine in Somalia and the Congo, Baby Doc's fall in Haiti, the sex trade in Bangkok, the AIDS battle in Central Africa, the Israeli bombing of Lebanon and Gaza, the Arab Spring revolt in Egypt, and the conflict in central Ukraine. This thing in Sudan is a piece of cake."

As I watched her, I summed her up. She was a prime example of the whites in action in Africa, who were living up to the dream of themselves in the golden days of colonialism. They were entitled because they were white, and they were never stopped by their darker brothers or questioned. I remembered my travel to Sudan just a few days ago. I had discovered that as a black man, I was not afforded that privilege. Even yesterday I had determined that someone had gone through my luggage, searching for who knew what.

"Elsa, you think a lot of yourself," Addie finally said.

Again, the raucous laughter. Nawara joined in for once and giggled, knowing that my Southern gal had struck home.

"Honey chile, I'm not a shrinking violet," our British buddy said, doing her imitation of a gum-smacking homegirl.

Nawara turned her attention to me again. "You would think that the West would throw in the towel. Elsa, did I say that right?"

"Yes, you said it right. A perfect Yank expression."

"You would think the West would feel like a fool for all the money and technology it has pumped into Africa over the course of so many years," Nawara said harshly. "What do they have to show for it? Nothing."

The tension was thick. Both Addie and Nawara expected me to answer the question. It was a trap. My answer would initiate a lengthy argument, which I did not want to have at this time of the morning.

Elsa saved the day. "Nawara, you know the Yorkie pup I just bought in the Netherlands? I've always envied women who had children and that mothering instinct. Sophie—that's the Yorkie's name—got out of the yard one day through some hedges and got lost. It was like losing a child. I was so distressed. I cried and cried and cried. Thankfully, I found her."

Nawara gave her a bewildered look.

"I give her so much love, and she gives it back," Elsa added, almost weeping like a sentimental animal lover. "She's the sweetest dog. Everyone in my district simply loves her. She's a part of my family."

Addie seemed perplexed. But I knew what Elsa had just done. She'd done an end run to eliminate any possibility of a battle royal.

"I have always wondered why dogs sniff other dogs' behinds," our BBC pal joked. "Even my sweet little dog does it."

Nawara had had enough of this canine chatter. She wanted to get down to business, to discuss the logistics of our Sudan journey, the nitty-gritty of our travel to the refugee camps. After her little ASPCA stunt, Elsa got serious. She explained what awaited us: a short flight in a prop plane to the southern frontier, a hazardous road to the two Doctors Without Borders sites, a hard trek with convoys carrying USAID food and supplies to the camps, and a final destination at one of the big refugee facilities in rebel territory. Both Addie and Nawara took notes, filling up pages with important facts and figures.

"Now we're rockin' and rollin'," I shouted, turning the heads of the other guests in the lobby. This was truly the start of our Sudan adventure.

8

TO REPAY A DEBT

While the others went back upstairs, I stepped out of the hotel and saw that the two security guys were still present, along with three government soldiers carrying weapons. They were keeping an eye on our little party. We were going to depart Khartoum in two days, but that wasn't quick enough for me. In the United States, I was sure the authorities watched you, but they never made it so obvious. Possibly, it was the fear that you were under a microscope that made you toe the line, be well behaved, and refrain from try anything illegal.

The blistering African sun rained its scorching heat down on the city. I looked up, felt the sweat sticking to my shirt and underarms, and started walking in the direction of the market I'd passed on my way to the hotel. Suddenly, Elsa ran up, waving her arms, shouting that there was a protest scheduled near the eastern part of the city.

"Where's Addie?" I asked, wanting her for company.

Elsa smirked. "She didn't feel well. Tummy trouble."

She gave me a big bag containing her cameras and lens, then shoved me in the car that she'd flagged down. Once we were both in the backseat, I noticed that she'd tucked her hair under a Yankee baseball cap. Her face was covered with nervous sweat from the adrenaline rushing through her sturdy limbs, though she was eager to capture the turmoil of the protest. I looked out the back window and noticed that the two security guys were tailing us in a car but keeping a respectable distance.

"Where's your Egyptian friend?" I asked curiously.

"She went to bed. She's getting some needed sleep, because we were out late at one of the cafés last night." Elsa chuckled. "She's not used to this hectic pace like I am."

"Who's protesting?"

Her eyes, bloodshot from fatigue, narrowed. "These are the same people who protested last fall against the twenty-four-year regime of President Omar al-Bashir. They know he's a tyrant. They're also angered by his cuts in fuel and gas subsidies, because nobody can run a home or business with the government mucking in their affairs. I've wondered why the Sudanese people have not risen up before now. They have had good examples of popular revolts against dictatorships in the Arab world in the past two years. You know, the Arab Spring?"

I nodded knowingly. "Sheep will always remain sheep."

"Speaking of sheep . . . can I ask you a question?" she said, fumbling with a lens on her Nikon camera, which she'd pulled out of the bag. "Why do you drag yourself around with that country bumpkin? She brings nothing to the party. She has the intellect of a bag of rocks."

Her question caught me off guard. "I like her. I'm here because of her. She got me out of the doldrums, got me to get off my butt and get back involved in the world."

"So?" Elsa was not having it. Addie was a bore in her mind.

"I owe a lot of positive things in my life to Addie," I said with sincerity. "She's from the country, but I find that refreshing. I don't have to worry about her pulling some devious tricks on me, betraying me. She speaks her mind. She's almost honest to a fault. I like that."

Elsa placed the camera back in the bag as the car weaved in and out of the traffic. "Clint . . . Can I call you Clint?"

"Yes. Sure." Just then I smelled a really rancid odor coming in the windows. It smelled like something had died and had not been buried.

She pulled out a cigarette, lit it, inhaled, and let the smoke slowly trickle out of her nostrils. "Clint, you'll get used to the smells. There are a lot of unusual odors over here, not like what one would smell in New York or London."

The driver, a Muslim, waved his hand to chase away the cigarette smoke that was filling the car. I didn't mind. As a former smoker, I often fought the urge to return to smoking. A tobacco addiction was one more thing I had to keep out of my life. *Say no to smoking, right?* I thought.

Elsa thought for a moment and then asked if I was thinking of marrying Addie. I had considered that possibility. She wanted a real relationship, a legal marriage. However, the disaster of my first marriage had always hindered me from making any such move. I never wanted to go through that again.

"I don't know," I confessed.

"Have you been married before?"

She was getting very personal. White folks were always up in your business. They wanted to know everything about you, but they told you nothing about themselves. I wished our destination was closer so I wouldn't have to go through this police grilling.

"Yes."

"And what?" She was very nosy.

"It was hell. It ended badly. What about you? Have you ever been married?"

She smiled mysteriously and reached for another cigarette. I guessed this was a sore spot for her. Her eyes softened with emotion; then they became hardened.

"Elsa, have you been married?" I repeated.

She looked bored with the topic. Clearly, she wasn't listening anymore. Her fingers brought the cigarette to her thin lips, and she blew smoke ring after smoke ring into the car.

As she'd shown in the episode in the hotel lobby, Elsa controlled everything, manipulated the conversation, choosing what she wanted to discuss and what she did not. As far as I was concerned, I didn't care that she wanted to dominate the situation. But I wondered what she would do if she was no longer in control, if she had to submit to another person's will. How would she act?

After knocking on the partition, Elsa asked the driver if he knew where Street 60 on the east side of the city was. He grinned, showing a row of yellow teeth, and replied that he did.

"The Sudanese economy isn't worth a plugged nickel," she said, tossing the cigarette out the window. "It's been tanking, especially since the south broke off and became an independent state in twenty eleven. That's why there is so much trouble down there. It's all about money, I think. Yes, the tribal and ethnic thing plays into the crisis, but the pressing issue is the oil. The government wants to get that moneymaker back."

I played along with her game. "When did al-Bashir take command of the country?"

"He headed a military coup back in nineteen eighty-nine. Since that time, his troops and their rebel cronies have practiced genocide in the western region of the country, Darfur. The West has complained about it, and the International Criminal Court even issued an arrest warrant for al-Bashir, but the man is still in control, and the body count goes higher."

"You better watch what you say," the driver warned, speaking in broken English. "You can get in trouble here."

"Piss off, man," the BBC reporter hissed.

When we got near the protest site, we saw buses packed with demonstrators carrying signs, young and old, with padding on their arms and knees. Protesters poured from cars on the side streets. There was a definite energy among them. They seemed determined, as if they were not going to back down in their opposition to the corrupt regime of al-Bashir.

"Oh yes, this is going to be fun," Elsa said, cheering. "The people will not be stopped. I don't know if you saw in the newspapers that the security forces have rounded up nearly one thousand activists, opposition members, journalists, religious types, and others in a sweep to crack down on dissent. Unfortunately, the government, which is Muslim, especially hates Christians, and that's you."

I watched the lines of marchers running toward the confrontation, eager and willing, determined to take a few blows to make their point. Surprisingly, a number of teens joined them, armed with nothing but their cell phones, to record the abuse that would be heaped on them. It was incredible to see them smiling and happy about going against the almighty protectors of the regime.

"Who are the bad guys?" I asked. "I want to know the score."

"It's Sudan's National Intelligence and Security Service who are keeping a lid on things," she explained. "They've got a lot of dissidents behind bars, where they beat and torture them, and keep them incommunicado, without access to their lawyers or their families."

I was stunned. "Are those guys following us in the National Intelligence and Security Service?"

"Probably," she answered drily.

Frightened, the driver let us off three blocks from the demonstration, suggesting that we walk the rest of the way. When we turned around, the driver was already backing up. Then he revved the engine and pulled down a side street. Nudging my arm, Elsa pointed to where the car that had been following us was parking at the curb. We watched as the two men who'd been inside it shoved their guns under their jackets, then ran to catch up with us.

9

WONDERLAND

Up ahead, the street was lined with two platoons of soldiers in riot gear, weapons and tear gas at the ready. Behind them stood three trucks of thugs wielding batons and clubs, prepared to punish and break bones and heads. I saw nearly fifty plainclothes officers standing near two armored cars, holding firm as replacements if the crowd got really out of hand, if the advantage of superior force couldn't smash the protesters.

"Oh yes, oh yes. Let's get it on." Elsa chuckled, the joy upon her, as if she were a new religious convert. "President al-Bashir cannot say he's honoring the right to freedom of expression and assembly. All lies. They want to break some heads, make some arrests."

This was like the infamous march in Selma or Birmingham, with Dr. King and his followers going head-to-head against the bigoted cracker sheriff, his armed redneck men, the powerful fire hoses, the vicious police dogs. I watched their stoic faces. They were unafraid. Their courage made you proud and humble.

"I think the villains are going to give them a bad time," I said, seeing the soldiers lift their tear-gas guns.

Elsa looked me in the eye, inspired, too, by their bravery and boldness. "These people have got to do this, because if they don't, the regime will never end," she said. "Al-Bashir's henchmen are taking them from their homes and arresting them at their jobs. No warrants at all. The president means business. He's not going to give up without a fight, not like Mubarak in Egypt."

The rows of security forces prepared for the thousands of protesters marching toward them, taking a defensive stance, watching the stragglers on the sidewalks. Some of the men and women clutched pipes, rocks, and bottles. Other specially equipped troops were suspiciously eyeing the demonstrators who had blocked the street with hastily constructed barriers to keep out reinforcements. Their signs read DOWN WITH THE REGIME! and PRESIDENT AL-BASHIR MUST GO!

"The government orders you to stop where you are, and if you do not, then we will be forced to disperse this crowd," one man, with a chest full of military medals, yelled through a bullhorn. "We do not want to use extreme measures, but we will. Anyone who will not leave the area will be subject to criminal and disciplinary proceedings. Leave!"

Suddenly, someone threw a rock at the Plexiglas shields of the soldiers, who then struck aggressive poses with their batons and moved forward in a resounding military lockstep. One more rock followed that one, and then another and another. Soon the young demonstrators were hurling bottles from all directions at the security forces, shattering glass on top of the vehicles and sending shards into the men cowering behind open doors. Elsa pulled me by the arm and yelled that this was a repeat of the clash at the University of Khartoum, when students faced off against the police and National Security and Intelligence Service officers. The noise was deafening. There were screams, shouts, shrieks, loud whistles, and pounding on pans.

"The government will not ask you again!" shouted the man with the bullhorn. "This is unlawful assembly. Leave! Leave! What is this going to accomplish? Nothing!"

In a few minutes, a sixth of the protesters had fallen, and now the battle lines were drawn. The soldiers stepped over the dead and the wounded, slashing their batons at the men and women, who retreated as fast as they could. On the sidewalks, several of the soldiers charged into the crowd, smashing bodies with their reinforced batons, clubbing them with their weapons, stomping on and kicking the fallen between cars. I smelled the harsh odor of tear gas as three of the soldiers stepped forward and fired rubber bullets at the throng, knocking the marchers to the ground, injuring them in the face, neck, and stomach. Screaming at the soldiers, a few of the brave dragged the injured into the center of the crowd of protesters, where they tended to their wounds. From there they took the injured to cars on the edges of the protest.

"Did you see that soldier kick the woman while she was crawling?" Elsa said above the roar of the angry crowd. "Things are really getting out of control!"

A group of protesters smashed windows in the buildings on the street, while others turned over several cars and torched them with kerosene. Elsa pointed out the people who belonged to the opposition party known as the Umma Party, adding that the soldiers were targeting them with a shower of rubber bullets and directing more tear gas into that area. An officer waved to the thugs in the trucks and sent them storming into the crowd of protesters, who resisted them with fists against clubs but then relented given the sheer number and the violence of the troops. They punished the protesters, the clergy, the reporters, the cameramen, and the photographers alike. Watching the marchers drop one after another made me tremble with fear. Everybody was fair game.

"They're smashing the cell phones of the kids so they will not post videos on Facebook," Elsa said during a brief lull in the action. "They do not want news of the government's harsh treatment of these people to get out to the world. This is happening here and in seven other cities in the country."

There was total bedlam. The soldiers who had been behind the trucks and armed cars were now chasing down the marchers, beating them where they stood or where they were hiding between buildings or cars. With rifles drawn, they ordered a number of the protesters to their knees and told them to put their hands behind their backs. Some of the other protesters tackled the soldiers to prevent the arrested men and women from being loaded into the trucks. The soldiers retaliated by yanking women by their hair, slamming them into the sides of the vehicles, punching them in the face until they were bloodied, and throwing them cruelly onto the concrete. The men and boys suffered an even harsher punishment. More rocks and bottles sailed through the air, and chants of "No high prices" and "No corruption" rang out, as young and old, their voices hoarse, demanded justice.

Behind us, tires burned and more tear gas bellowed up from amid the protesters. More reinforcements for the government arrived, the frenzied bloodletting suddenly went up a notch, The soldiers cornered terrified running bodies to make mass arrests, and two gas stations were torched and began bellowing plumes of black smoke. In this chaos, soldiers fired live ammo, the shots ringing out in a series of booms.

"We're out of here!" Elsa started sprinting in the direction from whence we had come. "Keep your head down!"

I followed her as she dashed through the frightened mob, the protesters running frantically in different directions. The firing of live ammo continued with a *rat-rat-rat-tat-tat*. It was coming from the group of trucks on the side of the security forces. The living trampled the dead.

Elsa flagged down some friends in a bullet-pocked van. We climbed into the van and squeezed between the wounded protesters who were cowering between the seats. The van sped down narrow side streets, past police checkpoints, to the hotel.

10

TOO EARLY TO LEAVE

Drained from the experience of the protest, I staggered into my room, my heart pounding like a Zulu war drum, my mouth dry, my legs without strength. Elsa followed me into my room, overcome by what she had just witnessed. A damnable slaughter! A government massacre! She immediately cut on the radio and tuned it to a pirate station that was broadcasting about the protest. The man reading the newscast had a deep baritone voice. She translated his words for me as I put on some water for tea.

"Today's protests occurred in Khartoum, Omdurman, Burri, Al-Daim, El Obeid, and Sennar. The police and soldiers used extreme force during the clashes with protesters," the announcer intoned. "The marchers attacked the security forces with sticks and rocks, but they proved no match for the tear gas and live bullets. A large number of protesters were seriously injured, and many were killed, among them students and activists. The government has not released any list of the wounded or dead."

Elsa sat on a chair facing the window and lit a cigarette before checking on our friends in the street below. "We still have company. I'm not surprised that they haven't arrested us."

"Give them time," I wisecracked.

The BBC reporter motioned for me to cut the radio up, putting a hand to her ear. "An official with Amnesty International said the authorities must rein in the security forces to prevent them from using such excessive force, which is in violation of international law. He added that firearms should not be used to disperse demonstrations under the law. Also, he called on the government to launch an impartial investigation into the protests, to ensure that those who were responsible for such a loss of life be brought to justice."

Elsa roared with laughter, saying that it was a crock. "Nothing will be done. Reverend, you did all right out there. I thought you would panic and start to run, but you didn't. Proud of you."

I smiled weakly and continued making the tea. I didn't feel heroic.

"You don't have anything stronger than this tea," she said, frowning at the cups. "No, you wouldn't, would you?"

"No, I don't." I watched her smoke with her head thrown back.

"Reverend, I don't buy this religious tripe," she said. "Jesus or Allah. In my life, I've seen so much misery and suffering caused by religion. Look at the Middle East. Look at this place here. I know you believe, but everything in this world cries, 'No, there is no God.'"

I poured the hot tea into a cup for myself. "I've run into nonbelievers before. You'll never believe. You have a closed mind. That means you will dismiss everything that does not fit into your belief system."

"You're wrong there," she protested.

"I don't think so. If you can't see it, then you don't believe. You're prejudiced against religion. No amount of investigation of the facts would convince you of the existence of Jesus. Or even Allah."

"That's bull. If there was evidence that you could show me in this world, I'd become one of your biggest believers. You can believe that."

I searched around the cupboard for anything sweet for the tea. My fingers moved things around, but I found nothing.

Elsa was hammering away at the idea of a deity. "I'm right to be skeptical about Jesus. How can you believe in Him with the madness in the world? Humans live at a hectic pace, and they love to sin, have their vices, and kill. Nobody cares about a loving, merciful God. They don't act like it."

"Some of us do," I replied. "We know that if God didn't hold us in His grace, we would not survive."

She watched me find a saucer to place on top of the steaming cup. "Life goes by too quickly to believe in such rubbish. It's a fraud."

"Do you believe in miracles?" I asked.

"No, I don't," she said firmly. "Jesus did not rise from the dead. He did not heal the sick or resurrect the dead or turn water into wine. He was not a great magician, like in a circus or a carnival. He did not die for our sins, nor will He return to judge us for our sins."

"I'll continue to pray for you," I said, smiling.

Elsa gave me a sarcastic laugh, mocking my Christian generosity and evangelism, ridiculing my faith, like a good sinner should.

"Reverend, I know the Bible too," she said. "As a modern sinner, I'm pretty up to date. Supposedly, the Gospel accounts of Matthew, Mark, Luke, and John tell everything about Jesus's life and resurrection. The accounts differ greatly from each other. They're essentially tall tales, fantasy and myth."

Disgusted, I kept my mouth closed. I found a seat near her and sipped my tea. For several minutes, we remained silent, aware of the increasing tension between us, listening through the thin walls to people in the hallway talking in Arabic.

Elsa stubbed out a cigarette butt, and then she lit another cigarette. "Earlier, you asked me if I'd ever been married. To answer your question, yes. In fact, I'm still married to a Scotsman who is involved in the banking industry in London. He wants a divorce. I guess he doesn't love me anymore."

"Sometimes we let love die," I replied.

"Reverend, I work really hard as a journalist," she said sadly. "I come home after one of these butt-kicking assignments and find my prince of a husband hasn't done anything. He just stretches out on the sofa, smokes his cigar, and drinks whiskey. I resent that."

"Does he work hard too?"

She breathed out streams of smoke through her nostrils, like an upset dragon from a fairy tale, then said she realized he had a tough job. "I know he works hard too, but it's not like me doing the news. As you can see by what we did today, gathering news is not a lark. He accuses me of disregarding what he does for a living."

"Do you?"

Her head nodded. "There's no point to love or marriage."

"I'm sorry you feel that way, Elsa."

"My husband told his divorce lawyer that I always seemed angry at him, that I barked at him about everything, that I believed everything he did was wrong."

"Well, was he being truthful?"

"Reverend, maybe so, maybe not. He also told the lawyer that I was a nympho, that I wanted sex too much. Yes, he was good, but that was not his only talent. Toward the end, my husband burnt out sexually. White men often do. All I wanted was someone who wanted me, desired me, and thought I was hot."

"Desirable?" I mused at her romantic wish list.

"Yes, every woman wants that," she said, rolling her eyes. "But there were other things. He wasted our future. He wasted our money on drink and gambling. He wasn't really committed to the relationship anymore."

"How do you know he wasn't committed to it?" I was angry at how she made it all his fault. I wished I could hear his side of things.

Elsa dismissed me with a wave of her hand. "I no longer loved him. I didn't want to fix him. I just wanted to get away. It was over, finished."

I put on my philosophical hat, lecturing her about the obligations and responsibilities of marriage. "We have to face up to the vows. It means 'for better or worse' and 'til death do us part.' We have to endure the stress and anxiety at the lowest points in the marriage, while sticking to the vows of loyalty and trust."

"Marriage is a big lie, just like religion," she bellowed fiercely. "The truth of the good marriage is the opposite. You think the other person will change and things will get better. It's all a big lie. Things never get better. It never changes."

I continued to drink the tea. "I guess it all boils down to problem solving. Finding solutions. Finding options. Refusing to fail."

She grimaced at me and my rosy viewpoint. "Our relationship was too empty, too cold, too destructive. It was a dead marriage. You don't know what you're talking about. We did horrible things, horrible things, irresponsible things, to each other that put our marriage in jeopardy. We sent it over the cliff."

"And it is beyond repair? You cannot go back?"

"No, Reverend, the marriage is kaput," she growled. "The Bible doesn't tell you how to fall in love or how to sustain a dead marriage. Nothing in the holy scriptures tells you to learn to cope with the differences between you and your supposed soul mate.

"You're shameless and very selfish," I retorted.

"And you're a good man, Reverend," she said, smiling victoriously.

"Thank you, Elsa," I said, holding up my cup.

"I bet that's not all you're good at," she said, flirting.

Bone tired, I put the cup on the table and made a face that revealed my total disappointment with her. She was being a witch. Suddenly, I wanted to take a nap. I threw her out of my room. She was mad, but she left. What we didn't know was that Addie had been listening outside the room and was not pleased.

11

JUST A MOMENT

A short time after Elsa's departure, Addie knocked on my door, giving three loud knocks. When I opened it, she glared at me with daggers in her eyes, went to the chair, and sat with her accusing finger pointing at my face. She was wearing a white blouse and jeans, and she was sweating profusely. Her hair was down and tied off in a long ponytail. I could tell she had been storing all this tension and now she was going to let me have it.

"Clint, what are you doing?" she said with an edge to her voice.

By the way, Addie was wearing glasses. I'd never seen her in eyeglasses before, didn't know she wore them.

"What am I supposed to have done?" I asked.

Addie was furious. "What are you doing with Elsa?"

"Nothing. I know I've been spending a lot of time with her, but she knows everybody who is anybody. I have many questions, and she knows the answers to some of them. After all, this is her turf, and she knows the players well."

Her voice softened into a low moan. "You left me, Clint. You left me all alone. I didn't know where to find you. Looked all over for you."

"Elsa took me to one of the protests by Sudan's opposition," I said. "It was incredible. It reminded me of the civil rights marches in the sixties. I tell you, there is more to this country than is ever printed in the American media. A lot more."

"Clint, wasn't that dangerous?"

"Not really." To my surprise, she was really worried about something happening to me. I couldn't figure her out. She ran hot and cold in her feelings toward me.

Then Addie totally floored me when she said I was lusting after Elsa, this foreign white woman, and wanted to go off with her. She stared at me all the time she said this.

"We're doing nothing wrong, Addie," I said.

"I was standing outside the door and heard everything," she admitted. "I heard her talking to you, telling you intimate things. She has designs on you. She wants you to make love to her. You don't see it, but I do."

Addie was starting to get on my nerves. Her behavior was very peculiar. Why was she saying these things? Where was the free-spirited, spontaneous woman I met in Alabama?

"I assure you nothing happened," I replied. "Elsa told me that you were sick. I heard you had tummy trouble. Do you need a doctor?"

"It passed. Something I ate."

I stood there, defending myself against her jealousy. There had been nothing intimate between Elsa and me. Only a little innocent flirting, on her part. That didn't count.

"Let's go down to my room," she said, sniffing. "I can still smell her here. Her sour sweat. Come, my lusty pastor."

We made our way downstairs. Inside her cubbyhole-sized room, I gazed around and noticed the decor was very similar to mine. The air conditioner, like the one in my room, was barely operating. Still, it was better than being outside.

"All you need is a scandal over here, and you will never stand in the pulpit again," Addie remarked with venom. "Everything is sex to these women. You thought you had problems with your crazy wife and her actions. I don't think you've gotten over it. Maybe you just don't like black women."

I sat on her bed. "That's not the case."

"I'm a country gal, and I've seen things," she said. "White folk fear you mating with their women, but they're proud to say they slept with a black wench. They feel like a man if they do that. I recall my daddy saying he had to look the other way if a white woman walked by. If he didn't, that could cost him his life."

"Addie, that was years ago," I explained. "The world has loosened up since those horrible times. We don't have black bucks and mammies and coons anymore. Heck, we even have a black president."

"But that time is in my blood," she said. "I'm a product of the South and that tradition. Every black boy and man in the South knows about the wicked sexual appetite of the white woman. The sacred myth of the lily-white queen. Even now, they know that if you step out of line, you can get in trouble behind those pink ladies. It's the Southern way of life."

"Would you want your sister to marry a black buck?" I joked.

"Do you want a cold Coke?" she asked, ignoring my words.

"Sure. Where did you get them?"

"I just want to warn you about Elsa," she said. "Something's not right about her. I feel it. I saw how she was watching you, like she had a real bad hunger for you. I know her . . . that type. They don't like to hear the word *no*. She'd get off getting you to herself, and I don't want to see that happen."

"I never got that from her, any of that," I said.

"Clint, do you trust her?" She handed me the soda.

I drank some of it, It was very frosty. "I see nothing indicating I should beware."

"You're lying through your teeth, and you know it."

"No, no, no." This was getting nuts.

She picked up a blouse that was hanging over a chair, as she'd just washed it, and put it on a hanger. "Elsa's all about herself. She doesn't care at all about us, except about getting you alone."

"She had me alone," I countered. "Nothing happened."

"What do you think she wants?" she asked.

"I don't know."

"What do *you* want, Clint?" She stopped and looked at me.

"All I want is a quiet and productive life," I said. "I want to forget the past. I want to live in the present. I want to enjoy Africa and Sudan. I want you to enjoy it as well."

She walked into the bathroom, ran cool water over her face. "I wonder how many black lovers she has had. Probably too many to count."

When she came back into the room, she was still jabbering away on the "Elsa the tramp" theme. "Elsa's thinking of you only in sexual terms. You're just a conquest, a notch on her belt. I'm sure she doesn't want to live with you in London. Her family and friends would probably abandon her. The men would label her a slut or worse."

I leaped up, spilling the soda. "Stop this! I knew you could be jealous, but this is going too far. Enough is enough."

She stepped up to me, her face close to mine. "Maybe I should take my black butt back to Alabama. At least black people know what's what. You can ignore this warning, but Elsa is up to no good. She's gonna hurt you. Watch and see."

Fed up, I left her room and went downstairs to the lobby, where Elsa was surrounded by a group of big black men and was smiling and laughing as she poked at a small black puppy. The reporter lifted the puppy up and yelled, "His name is Clint." They all laughed loudly. I went upstairs, insulted and humiliated, and thought about what Addie had said.

Addie was a country gal, but a wise country gal.

12

NO SMOKE WITHOUT FIRE

It took me about twenty minutes to arrive back at my place. Twenty minutes! I left enough time for any kind of search of the premises. I knew what I would find. My room was in shambles. Possibly someone from the Sudan's National Intelligence and Security Service trashed my room, searched through everything, every nook and cranny. I wondered what they were looking for.

Word came some time later that day that a man from Carter would take us to a nearby airport, where we would board a cargo plane that would carry us south. Elsa delighted in the fact that we were leaving Khartoum, because she was concerned that the protests might consume her time in Sudan and she wanted to get out of the city to cover the front lines of the conflict. Addie avoided me until it was time to go. As Elsa's guest, Nawara, the young Egyptian woman, would be along for the dangerous ride. She had been acting very mysterious, sometimes keeping company with government officials during the day, worshipping with the radicals at the mosque, and dragging Elsa to various secret clubs and dives in the city's underground.

Before I took the next step in my Sudan adventure, I got a call from the editor, Hasseem, who warned me not to think badly of his country based on what I was about to witness in the south. He also told me that he doubted that I, a man of God, would be able to reconcile the violence and bloodlust of the territories of the Christians with the good words of the holy scriptures.

"Believe me, I was the government's friend and ally," Hasseem said. "I defended them and their barbaric actions when no newspaper would come out to stand for them. I called for closer economic ties with the Jews in the newspaper and on TV. What did I get for my trouble?"

"I don't know," I answered. "What?"

The editor snorted angrily before beginning his tirade. "A gang of thugs, all in masks, crashed into my office and beat up my staff yesterday. Slapped the receptionists. Then they punched and kicked me, tossed me on the floor, and whipped me with their pistols. I didn't deserve this."

"Some government men have been following me since my arrival," I replied. "I'll be glad to get out of this blasted place."

A cough followed my fearful statement. "Also, security forces confiscated our newspapers from the plant, and officials told us to suspend production, unless we could follow their lead," Hasseem said. "They said the government did not want to discipline us further or impose security restrictions on the press. I got their message."

"Are you closing down?" I asked.

"I'll lose so much money that I won't be able to publish," he said. "Three of my reporters have been arrested. They're being held somewhere without charge. We've not been able to locate them."

We both paused to let the warning he'd received sink in my head. If they would step on the neck of a longtime friend, what would they do to me? It would be very easy for them to make me disappear. They could kill me, and nobody would ever know.

"The government knows all your plans," Hasseem said with amusement. "They know everything. I told you this before. I was talking to someone at the *Times* in London, and he advises you not to go to Darfur, the Abyei region, the Blue Nile state, Southern Kordofan, or any area near the White Nile south of the Kosti–El Obeid–En Nahud road. There is so much rebel activity there. You can be killed."

It was my time to swallow from fear. "Attacks from the various militias happen all the time," I said. "I know this, but I want to see firsthand the humanitarian crisis that is there."

The editor laughed rudely. "Another nosy American. Remember the places I just told you. They kill foreigners there. Stay away from there."

"Nothing will deter me from going out there," I said boldly.

I could see in my mind's eye Hasseem shaking his head before saying that this fact-finding journey would change me forever. And then he chuckled and hung up.

13

TOO LATE NOW

It was a rush job. Everything was supposedly hush-hush, but Sudanese intelligence knew the whole deal, from top to bottom. Hasseem had warned me that we couldn't pull the wool over their eyes. I tried to remain cool, but my mind was full of doubt and worry. Addie played the strong heroine, walking with her head held high, even though I knew she was having second thoughts about coming to Sudan.

"What's up?" I greeted as Elsa walked past me in the hallway outside my hotel room. We were headed to the lobby, as we would soon be on our way to the airport.

She wore the tightest pants I'd seen since I left the States. No panties. She pranced down the hallway, carrying her BOAC shoulder bag and a couple of cameras. She ignored me. That was all right with me.

We barely had time to get everything together before our departure, since Carter whisked us out to the van. Elsa had cautioned me about Carter and his urgent attitude. Everything was hurried with him, and if you couldn't keep up, you got left behind. Finally, we were all in the van and heading, with utmost haste, to the remote airport. I noticed that the car containing the Sudanese security guys was not around. Addie realized that too and wondered aloud whether the officials had called them off because we were leaving and we would be someone else's headache.

Carter drove like a maniac, running red lights and blazing down side streets. Everybody was nervous. But nobody said anything. Elsa finally told him that he was going to draw attention to us and that we'd get stopped by the police.

"Go. Go faster," said Nigel, his sidekick. It seemed he was a reckless man and did not care about the consequences of his actions.

Elsa informed us that Carter and Nigel had a running joke about the long arm of the security forces. "Bumbling Keystone Cops," they called them. Still, the pair worked their plan to perfection, getting us and their men in a dead run onto the tarmac and then onto the plane, which lifted off before the control tower could be alerted and then, after an hour and a half, settled down on a makeshift airstrip, where it was met by a trio of trucks packed with desperately needed supplies and more armed men. The supplies were loaded onto the plane after it landed and the armed men filed in.

Once we were airborne again, our group laughed and joked, feeling smug in the plane, while the mercenaries smoked quietly and watched us with bemusement.

"Pray for us, Reverend," said one pasty-faced man in combat fatigues while he took his weapon apart systematically.

Glancing at the gunmen sitting on the far side of the plane, I joked and gave them the symbol of the cross, like a pope, but when that gesture fell flat, I knelt and folded my hands in prayer. Some of Carter's men followed suit, but not Elsa, Nawara, and the group of burly thugs who had just got on the plane.

"Are you Catholic?" another mercenary asked, pulling a glowing cigarette to his mouth in the dimly lit cabin. "They told me you were Baptist. Right?"

I nodded.

His superior was tired of this boring spiritual banter and asked if the arms, ammo, and supplies had been loaded. "Affirmative," two guys answered at once. To make the flight go smoothly, the necessary government officials had been slipped bribes to silence them.

I glanced over at Addie. She looked pale. "What's wrong?" I asked her.

"Nothing, Clint," she replied hastily, then asked for a cigarette from one of the gunmen. He lit one for her, flirting with her, making seductive eye contact with the country gal, then handed it over.

I noticed that few of the gunmen pretended to smile at me. *A meek lamb thrown in among wolves.* The taut expressions on their pale faces told me that I made them extremely uneasy. They were worried that I'd just get in the way. It was up to me to make myself scarce.

"What are you going to do down there, Minister?" their superior quizzed me with veiled eyes.

"Offer a hand and possibly some hope," I replied, feeling their faces turned toward me.

They laughed as a group, mocking me. One man, who was quite large, shouted that they needed not prayers or hymns but blasted guns. If they had those guns, the militias would steer clear of them. The large man stood, adjusting his automatic and shaking his head. The entire team agreed with him. They believed that only force could trump force.

With the metallic hum of its mighty engines, the plane sailed over an endless stretch of reddish-brown sand, dotted occasionally by villages, which had probably been there for generations. I sat away from the window, breathing in the warrior sweat and the oil fumes. Wiping her forehead, Addie slumped against the wall. She looked sick.

"Can I get you something, honey?" Elsa asked her.

Addie, appearing about to faint, waved her off and said, "Just feeling fine."

Elsa turned in her seat to face the commander. Then she asked him, "Are you fellows going down there with us?"

"Negative." He was not risking his men or his arms on a lark.

"Can you send a couple of your men to accompany us to the camps?" she persisted.

"Negative," the big man repeated.

"Please, please, please," Elsa said prettily, battling her eyes like Gidget.

That softened him up a bit. "Okay. Two. Just until you people get to the camps. Then they get the first thing smoking out. No delays. You forget Carter has men under his command. They're very capable fighting men."

The plane started to descend, circling, circling, circling, until it made its final approach. It bounced once, twice, on the landing. When it stopped on the hardened clay runway, crowds of people ran toward it, yelling and shouting. The mercenaries stood, checked their weapons, and marched off the plane to meet their audience. Carter motioned for us to remain on the plane until everything was secure and safe. The mercenaries unloaded some of the supplies, as per their agreement, onto the trucks waiting at the rear of the aircraft. Two sentries were posted on each side of the trucks, guns at the ready, watching the tall grass for intruders.

"Take care," the commander instructed, as we got off the plane. "This is enemy territory. It'll be nightfall soon. You probably better make camp here and post guards. Then we'll press on to the Doctors Without Border camp before dawn tomorrow."

The commander shook Carter's hands, then Nigel's, and then the big man gave Elsa a bear hug, which she enjoyed. With the supplies offloaded, the plane turned around, its engines revved up, and it sailed off into the golden sunset.

When some of the refugees who had gathered on the runway learned that I was a minister, they crowded around me, asking for my blessing and comfort. I realized my Lord had spared my life in Alabama so that I could reach this day and show these people that God had not abandoned them, that God saw them and had not forgotten them. With each hug and touch, I wanted to convince them that the power of God was at work even in this darkest of moments.

"Oh, you're doing your Billy Graham thing," Elsa joked as I walked among the hungry and raggedy survivors. "I'm watching you. You're very good at this. I like to see you pour it on." I learned that some of the refugees had been walking for days and even weeks, avoiding the enemy forces, who were looting, killing, and destroying villages in their path. They'd known that their homes and villages were unsafe, for the enemy had sworn to wipe them out. As they'd fled into the bush, they'd heard agonizing screams for help, heard the gunshots, seen the smoke and fire that consumed their homes, and smelled the sickening odor of burning human flesh. They'd remained out of sight, hoping the invasion would end, waiting until the violence passed. But it hadn't passed, and so the refugees had fled, without food or water, into the unfriendly darkness to escape death. Nobody had wanted to die, and that was what the enemy had offered—convert to Islam or die. Renounce Jesus Christ, the religion of the oppressors. Come home to Islam. Or die. So here they were at the camp, under our protection, eating the food and drinking the water at an alarming rate because of the heat. This place, as one of the people told me, could get to 130 degrees at midday.

While we set up camp—five tents surrounded by sentries—Carter told us the enemy was out there, watching us from afar, moving around to get into position. He cautioned us to stay close to the camp. Knowing the enemy was so close gave me a creepy feeling. The refugees huddled inside the perimeter of the camp, dropping their weary bodies into any space that could accommodate them. The lucky ones needed medical attention for minor ailments, but the unlucky were in bad shape and nothing could be done for them. The women tried to make them comfortable.

"Do you know how to use a gun?" Carter asked me after we set up camp.

"Yes. My father took me hunting when I was little," I replied.

"Well, if things get serious, we might have to call upon you for help," he said. "The enemy will have no mercy, especially for you, a messenger of Jesus Christ. I hope we can call on you if it gets bad. I hope it does not."

With a shrug, he put a .45 automatic pistol in my hands. I smiled weakly, knowing that I could not give in to any feelings of panic or anxiety. This was no time to be scared. When the night came, I drew strength from the quiet moments, from my observations of the women scurrying among the survivors, the staff bandaging cuts and scrapes, and the men patrolling the boundaries of the camp.

Addie was avoiding me. Every time I saw her, she wore a sour face. Also, she was smoking cigarettes, a new habit for her, and sitting with the fellows, drinking warm beer and laughing. She made sure that I noticed her. Her blouse was open provocatively, exposing more cleavage than usual. She was like a cat that had been let outside, an animal in heat.

Elsa saw this "cat on a hot tin roof" routine and commented that the country gal was on the prowl. "How does this make you feel?" she asked me as we watched Addie mingle with the fellows loading supplies on the trucks .

"Addie is a grown-up, and she can do whatever she wants," I remarked smugly. "I hope she knows what she's doing. These boys play rough."

"Maybe she just wants to make you jealous," the reporter suggested, squatting next to me.

"I've done nothing to make her jealous," I retorted.

"We know that, but she doesn't know anything," she said, clearly enjoying the fact that Addie was looking this way.

I stretched out, crossing my legs. "What a day!"

She laughed knowingly. "The best is yet to come."

There were only two fires in the camp, and they were kept low. Everything was pitch black, so I watched the shadows move through the area. A few minutes later Elsa got to her feet and started walking toward Nigel, who was holding out an aluminum pan to her. It contained beans and chunks of goat meat.

As she neared him, a single gunshot sounded from the darkness. Nigel fell forward into her arms, a horrible wound in his neck, and splattered blood all over her. Like many of those who were nearby, I rushed to them. Elsa watched Nigel's hopeless eyes, then opened up his collar to reveal an injury that was more serious than we had expected. A bright red spray of blood came from the wound.

Carter, his close friend and assistant, knelt beside him and checked his pulse. "He's gone. Elsa, can you get a blanket to cover him?"

I touched Carter's arm, my face showing pity and compassion. "Can I say a few words over him?"

Carter patted the head of his fallen friend and said that Nigel would like that. While the members of the camp, our refuge, bowed their heads in prayer, I spoke of a soul now departed from this life, awaiting the blessed redemption of the Master, and of the good deeds of the man, who had fought so that these people would have the right to worship.

Then two men carried Nigel's body into one of the tents. Elsa bent down and whispered reassuring words in Carter's ear. Her uniform still sported the crimson stains. Everybody went back to their places to wait for sunrise. No one was safe.

"The enemy has got his blood quota," Carter said to me sadly. "He won't mess with us any more tonight. Tomorrow is another day, and time is on his side. He knows this. But God will not be denied."

14

A HYMN TO THE SPIRIT

After Nigel's death by a sniper bullet, the enemy let our vehicles pass to the Doctors Without Borders camp, although we saw them shadowing us in the darkness, occasionally giving out grotesque bird cries. We carried Nigel's body in the rear of a Land Cruiser, wrapped securely in a blanket, almost like a corpse cocooned in solemn Islamic white. The caravan pulled up into a clearing carved out of the trees and bush. In the clearing were ten hastily built all-weather tents; two large buildings, where the staff lived; and four sheds containing the camp vehicles. Men armed with automatic weapons stood guard on towers surrounded by barbed wire.

It was daybreak when we were greeted warmly by Drs. Bromberg and Arriale, who shook our hands, then turned their attention to the medical supplies. For some reason, Elsa stayed outside when they showed us into one of the staff buildings. Everybody but Carter sat down, resting their weary bones.

Saddened by his friend's death, Carter informed the doctors that the enemy was just outside the camps, well armed and numbering about forty men.

"I'm so sorry about your loss," Dr. Bromberg said, tugging on the stethoscope around his neck. "He was a good man. Did a lot of good. We'll miss Nigel."

Carter allowed his body to sag as he leaned against the door. He seemed on the verge of tears, but that was not possible. He had cried when his loyal friend stopped breathing last night. Suddenly, Elsa walked into the place like she was royalty, straight from Buckingham Palace, and ordered the staff to put her luggage in a room.

"Where's the food, Doc?" she asked. "I'm famished."

Dr. Arriale, the taller of the two men, spoke with authority in a quiet voice. "Someone will get you something. What we are concerned with right now is the fact that a couple of villages were attacked last night. We're still counting the dead and dying."

"Are there any government troops in the area?" Carter asked.

"Or UN peacekeepers?" Elsa asked, reaching for a cigarette.

I kept my eye on Addie, who seemed completely distracted. She was still stunned by the sudden demise of Nigel, who had been gunned down in an instant. I could tell she was really having second thoughts about this trip. Elsa had told me that Addie was weighing the idea of going back to the States before the journey took a tragic turn. The country girl had not talked to me since our blowup in her room.

"What are your qualifications, Doc?" Elsa asked, without her tape recorder or her pen and notebook at the ready.

Dr. Bromberg walked over near the barricaded windows and spoke in a low, clear voice. "I got my schooling at Johns Hopkins, while some of the others trained at Mayo Clinic and Cleveland Clinic. One of my surgeons attended Columbia and NYU. We've got an eclectic bunch of medics here. Come on. Follow me. I'll show you around."

When they left the room, I trailed behind them, remaining just within earshot. I watched through an open doorway as several staff members herded some of the refugees into the tents and carried others who were too weak to walk any longer. The critically wounded were loaded onto stretchers and lugged into the makeshift clinics for treatment. Those who were stronger and were able to work lifted boxes and equipment, stacked them in front of the sheds, and waited for other orders.

"The reason the rebels tolerate us is that we don't choose sides," Dr. Bromberg explained. "We're simply neutral. We're in the business of patching people up and saving lives. About six days ago, there was a fierce firefight not that far away from here, uh . . . wounded on both sides. It turns out that some of the injured were from the rebels. The refugees recognized them, but they didn't say anything. And we didn't say anything, either."

Just then Elsa noticed me lurking, listening. "But isn't that permitting the bloodbath to continue? These are killers, cold-blooded killers, and you patch them up. Isn't that odd, Doc?"

"Not really," the doctor replied.

Elsa proceeded to butter him up. "They told me about you, how you were an amazing fellow. They told me you were the one to meet."

A staff member whispered to him about the supplies, the shortage of antibiotics and bandages, and the fact that the camp needed approval to build another shed for storage. Balding and short, Dr. Bromberg flashed an easy grin and touched the staff member on the shoulder.

"Great. We'll work that out with the camp administrators," he said. "CARE is sending us another doctor, one who worked in the war zone in Croatia and Afghanistan, and is capable in everything from surgery and maternity care to pediatrics. He's flying in from Nairobi the week after next."

"That's very good," Elsa said. "However, some of the media say camps like yours are good breeding grounds for the enemy. Do you agree with them?"

This was making the doctor uncomfortable. He just wanted to get this interview over with so he could get some rest. I knew all the medical staff worked ridiculous hours, put themselves in danger from both sides, and got very little financial compensation from anyone.

"Maybe you want to hear this, Reverend," the doctor said, waving me over to his side. "Elsa, you asked about whether we're breeding terrorists or the enemy in our camps. I say we are Christians and we are here for people who need us. We treat people who are sick, displaced, wounded, or dying."

Elsa looked serious. "Have you treated government troops?"

"Yes." The doctor glanced at me as he said this. I realized he was a man of deep faith, one who believed in the power of the Lord and everything that went into a follower of His word.

"That's insane," she countered. "The government is arming and financing the very people who are killing and raping the villagers you are treating and housing here. They are the real killers. They are the real plague in this area."

The doctor's face reflected his frustration with the reporter, for he knew that she would never understand how he could treat the enemies of his people, that she would never understand why the scriptures said that those who did good would receive blessings from the Lord.

"Like everybody here, we're in God's hands," he replied. "We're Christian healers. We hold fast to our faith in God. There are words of wisdom that I often recall by the writer Madora Kibbe. "Let Christian healers not be defined by sect and deed, but by word and deed.""

"What does that mean?" Elsa asked.

"It means just what we're doing at this camp," the doctor answered. "We're here to save lives. We're here to ease suffering."

I couldn't help but interrupt. "That's what I was trying to explain to you back in Khartoum. Christians obey the scriptures, which often call on them to take action against evil and suffering. I salute you, Doctor, for what you and your staff are doing."

Elsa was incensed, and she went on to recount atrocities and human rights violations she had witnessed while she had been in Sudan. She accused us of putting our heads in the sand while the bloodshed and slaughter continued. She thought it was sheer stupidity in the service of salvation.

"How can you be so blind!" she exclaimed. "Neither the government nor the rebels protect you. You're out here alone in the wind. They bombed the UN facilities the other day. They bombed two of the refugee camps in the border region last week. They slaughtered the inhabitants of five villages near here. In fact, didn't they strafe your camps last Easter?"

"That's true," the doctor grunted.

"How does your family feel about the work you're doing here?" Elsa quizzed.

Doctor Bromberg stared at the door that led outside, wishing he could leave right now.

"I said no personal questions," he replied tersely.

"What do you feel about South Sudan, Doctor?" she asked.

He moved toward the door, watching the long stream of refugees stagger through the medical compound and head to the camps beyond, weary and starved. What was the use? How many lives could they save? His explanation about Sudan and its liberation from colonialism in

1956 was something the reporter knew. The violent civil wars and the genocide that followed independence, and the truce between Khartoum and the southern rebels in 2005, didn't solve anything. The crisis exploded after South Sudan's independence in 2011, and the result was two million killed and hundreds of thousands maimed.

Refusing to be denied her story, Elsa said she knew the history of the region. She wanted his thoughts about the mortality rates in the refugee camps in South Sudan. Workers at one camp she'd visited in the Upper Nile area said they lost twelve children daily because of the shortages in supplies.

"What do you have to say about the high mortality rates, Doctor?" she asked.

"It's true about some of the camps, especially in the remote areas of the country," he explained, looking past her at the refugees marching past the building. "We lose a lot of them from preventable diseases, because of the crowded conditions and lack of medical supplies. We get cholera and other bad microbes from the contaminated water. Others suffer horrible injuries to their limbs from walking along roads filled with land mines. We treat plenty of these people who are just fleeing violence, trying to get food, water, and shelter. It's a shame."

"Do you think the world is tired of hearing all this bad news?" she asked. "It seems they've turned their attention elsewhere . . . to Kim K's fat butt or the tiff between Jay-Z and Beyoncé or the royal heir's first steps. With Africa, it's bad news all the time, and they're tired of it."

The doctor walked closer to the door and scratched his weary head. "That's probably why the funding for these places has fallen off," he suggested. "The world has a short attention span."

I took two steps toward him, hoping to divert his focus on how badly things were going around the camp.

"Has your Christian faith helped you in the business of healing?" I asked him, and his face lit up.

His smile was contagious. "Let me tell you something about myself," he said. "At first, I didn't believe in God. When I got accepted into medical school, I believed only in science and research. Through logic and reason, I'd argued against any kind of deity. I had several arguments against the existence of God, for I couldn't see anything positive in this uncivilized world. There was no God."

"What changed you?" I quizzed him.

"It didn't happen overnight," the doctor said. "After medical school, I did an internship in one of the teaching hospitals in the inner city. I had all kinds of proof that there wasn't any divine intervention in the affairs of humanity. The ghetto is a very hard place. As a white man, I wondered how people survived in that dismal environment, where disappointment and hate breed so rapidly."

I was a survivor of the ghetto. I had got out alive and had thrived, as many black and Hispanic people did. But I knew what he was saying as a white man. Looking at the "cullud" neighborhoods from the outside, I could see how he could come to this dismal conclusion.

"However, we shocked this black bus driver back to life, and I discovered that miracles do happen in this life," the doctor said excitedly. "He was dead, dead as a doornail. We worked on him for about thirty minutes. We were determined not to give up. And after three shocks, we got a pulse, at first faint, and then very strong. He was alive."

Elsa grimaced. She'd had enough of this spiritual talk.

The doctor continued, his words flowing out like those of a kid reciting an Easter piece. "I looked around and saw that some of the medical staff were praying for him to live. His family was outside, wringing their hands in fear. When I took my life over to Christ, I experienced

His power and grace. Finally, I understood the limits, the areas where modern medicine was ineffective, and discovered how divine grace can enter into a medical recovery. In my practice, I saw it every day. For instance, two people came in with the same disease, and one would die and the other would get well. We gave them the same treatment, but the results were different. Only God's grace can grant a miracle like this."

"I know what you mean," I agreed.

Elsa was fuming. "I don't. God doesn't have anything to do with it. It's fate. It's destiny. But it has nothing to do with God or Jesus or Allah."

The doctor shook his finger in her face and said that was not true. "Medical treatments, no matter how supposedly foolproof, often do not work," he asserted. "I see that in this camp, where life and death are in a constant battle. Elsa, you have no faith. But faith is important to physical healing. If you stick around long enough, I'll show you examples of faith at work."

"Faith involves the whole person—soul, spirit, and body," I said. "Christ's healing power cannot be denied. Prayer heals. It's not about false hope when you put yourself in God's hands."

Eventually, Elsa strutted outside, presumably, to get more local color. She was allergic to any talk of religion, spirituality, or God. We watched her through an open doorway as she talked with one of the soldiers, a big Dinka man in combat fatigues, with an automatic strapped to his waist.

"I'm glad you're here," the doctor said. "Elsa is wrong. You never know why healing doesn't occur in all situations. Every time I go into surgery, I know I must have faith in a good outcome, because all miracles begin with faith."

We went outside and stood watching the sad, unending parade. Suddenly, a young woman, a skeleton with skin stretched over it, stumbled up to us, one arm cradling a baby. Her other arm was a dark stump missing a hand. It had been hacked off, possibly with a machete. She moaned and then thrust the infant into my arms before she collapsed on the ground and died. The baby, sucking one finger, was nearly dead.

The doctor supervised the transport of the corpse to one of the sheds, handed the infant to one of his staff, and walked off with some of the other refugees. *God, protect these remarkable people,* I thought as the doctor hopped onto a truck headed to the main gate.

15

ODDS AND ENDS

The first thing I did the next day was find time for Addie. When I caught up with her, she was dressed in a short-sleeved blouse and khaki shorts. What I didn't like was that she had picked up a tobacco addiction. She now smoked about five cigarettes a day, and her fingers were now stained brown from the puffs she neglected to take while she chatted and from forcing fumes down her lungs. We sat near one of the medical tents, watching the sick and frail assisted to the road by staff to make way for others waiting for treatment.

"I want to go home," Addie said flatly.

"Why?" I knew that earlier in the week she'd been dissatisfied with this Sudanese journey and the amount of sickness and death it entailed.

"Clint, I didn't know it would be like this," she replied.

I shrugged that off. "Addie, you saw the slide show and heard the people talk about what was going on over here. They said it was heartbreaking and rather dangerous. They said Africa was dangerous. They said Sudan was dangerous. You knew this was not going to be a picnic."

She scowled at me. "I knew that, but you're ignoring me. You spend all your time with that white woman. I warned you about that. Did you see her with the big black soldiers? She's like a cat in heat. You know what she wants."

"Elsa will get nothing from me," I insisted.

"Are you sure, Clint?" She was lighting up another cigarette.

"Why are you smoking?"

Addie grinned. "I like it. Maybe it's because my folks didn't let me do it before. But I like it. It calms me."

I watched her inhale, then exhale, her nose shooting out snakes of smoke. "I don't plan to stay long, just long enough to see what I want to see. Bear witness. I think Americans, especially black Americans, should know what is going on in this part of the world. We watch the TV news, and this stuff is not really shown."

"Or it's shown when it gets really bad, Clint."

"Yes, you're right. But as I told Hasseem, the editor, I want to see for myself. This place is plain crazy . . . Africans killing Africans, Sudanese killing Sudanese, children of God killing each other. These people are killing women and children, effectively wiping out future generations. This is nuts."

"I know it is," she agreed.

For a moment, we listened to the steady sound of the big generators, which powered the refrigerators where the drugs were kept and the lights in the residences and the surgery tents.

"I'm lonely, Clint," Addie finally said.

I stepped back to let two men carry a man without legs to the tents so he could be treated. Bloody, dirty, and foul smelling. Addie shook her head in disbelief. Some of the other refugees walked toward the area where they would be counted, added to a list, and assigned space in the camps.

"Loneliness is something I know all about," I replied. "I lost my wife and kids. My wife killed the children too. I know I'm still not over it. This sense of loss still haunts me. Sometimes it drives me crazy. Sometimes I think I've found a cure for it, but then it comes back stronger than ever."

"You miss them, huh?"

"Yes. Lord knows I miss them, especially the kids." Addie lowered her eyes, with her hands covering her face. "Sometimes I miss my man too, even though he often treated me like a dog. I miss his touch. I miss the way he loved me. Why is that?"

"Dr. Smart used to say, 'Loneliness comes from being estranged from the Lord,'" I answered sadly.

"Estranged?" A puzzled expression appeared on her face.

"Separated. Alienated. That's what it means." I held her hand, her small one in my big one.

"Clint, maybe this whole trip to Sudan is about fear— fear of intimacy, fear of bringing somebody into my life. I don't want to end up an old maid. I want to start over, want to have a man of my own, want to start a family."

"Addie, I don't believe you'll end up an old maid," I said. "You've got too much going for you. I know you'll find somebody."

She freed her hand from mine, stood up, tossed a freshly lit cigarette butt, and stomped on it. Then she sat back down next to me. "I don't want to settle for just any-thing or just anybody. Putting a bandage on my broken heart is a phony, temporary cure. Do you know I mean?"

"I guess so. The late Dr. Smart also used to say that you could use loneliness as an emotional tool to get out of ruts and grow up. I think he had something there."

"Is Dr. Smart the one who tried to lead you astray?"

"Sorta. He did himself in with his own wickedness."

"You still respect him, don't you?" she asked.

I spoke as slowly and clearly as I could. "The dictionary defines *loneliness* as 'cut off from others,' 'being without company,' and 'feeling sad and blue.' I don't think the definition of *loneliness* fits us now. Look around you. We're in the middle of one of the world's hot spots, Sudan. I've never felt more alive."

Addie frowned at something I had said. "You said I'd find somebody. So what that means is it's not you. Right, Clint?"

"I don't know. I really don't know."

"Why don't you know, Clint? Why?"

I was suddenly irritated. "I followed you like an insecure puppy into this hellhole. Every devil is on the loose in this blasted place. I've seen things I wish I hadn't seen. This experience is extremely painful."

She stared at me cruelly. "But what does that have to do with me? You agreed to come. You're a grown-up. I didn't force you to come."

Immediately, I thought of something, and my mouth blurted out what my mind was thinking. "I wonder if Jesus was ever lonely. What do you think?"

"I don't know about that. That's more your business, your line of work." She reached for another cigarette from the pack, taking her time. I watched the men look at her, committing lust with their eyes. She loved the attention.

"Addie, do you often mistake quiet moments for loneliness? Do you get them mixed up?"

"No. I'm glad to be alone sometimes. It's good to just sit quietly, breathe, and read a nice book. Solitude is a good thing."

I sighed. "I'll tell you what. After all this is over, I'll enjoy my quiet time."

"I see your point," she said, laughing. "What about Elsa? Do you want to be with her?"

"All right, Addie. Do you want to chew me out over something I haven't done? Let's get it over with."

Her stance was bold and hostile. "Elsa is no good. She's no good for you. You see her flirting with every man she sees. I don't want you to be one of her victims."

"I'll remember that," I said curtly.

"What's to stop us from getting married?" she asked, looking deeply into my eyes.

It was my job to neutralize this blowup from the start with some common sense and plain speaking. She was trying to throw me off balance.

"I don't know if you want to marry me and go on the way we're going now," I said. "You don't know what you want. Now, you wanted to get me here so you could exercise some control over me. I was a fool. I should have never come here, but now that I'm here, I'm going to make the best of it."

She seemed offended. "You make me sound like an evil-minded heifer."

"Am I on the right track?" I asked. "Did you want me to follow you to Sudan so you could show me who is the boss?"

"No, Clint." Her answer was firm.

"Tell me the truth," I said.

She lifted her head proudly. "No, I didn't think that at all. I thought I had feelings for you at the time, and I wanted you to be near me. I wanted you to be with me."

"Are you sure that is all there was to it? Are you being truthful?"

"Yes," she said snidely. "That's all. I swear. I just wanted you to be with me. Now I know it was a big mistake. What do you think you're going to accomplish here?"

Somehow I resented her for asking me that question. She sounded like the editor and the government officials in Khartoum.

"I want to bear witness, to see this crisis up close and personal," I replied. "I want to know the facts and do good deeds in the name of the Lord. Sometimes I don't have to preach the Holy Word to these people. I just have to be a good example as the Lord's messenger."

"Clint, you'll get yourself killed," she said. "These people don't give a hoot about Jesus Christ or Christians. They want to wipe them out in Sudan."

"I know this," I said.

"So why put your neck out?" she asked.

"I read somewhere that 'God doesn't speak one language.' I can reach these sinners. Others have."

Interrupting our conversation, one of the staffers approached and gave me a jar of something, and I drank it down in almost one gulp. The stuff was fermented, frothy, tart, much like sweet ripe bananas.

"What is this?" I asked.

"Banana beer," he said, his dark face grinning, showing yellow teeth. "The doc felt you needed a drink after the long trip."

The staffer handed Addie a jar of the beer. She took one sip and then dumped the alien liquid on the ground. She screwed up her face, rolled her eyes at the Dinka staffer, and moved behind me when she noticed he was leering at her behind and legs.

16

NIGHTMARES SO REAL

I borrowed a newspaper from the doctors' residence and took it back to my tent. One of the stories caught my eye, the images of chaos and mayhem burning into my mind. The thought of whether this conflict would ever end troubled me. Violence was rampant and there seemed no way to stop it. Nobody had any answer or remedy for it.

White Nile, Sudan–(UPI)—Thousands of people have fled three villages in southern Sudan, where fierce fighting between local armed groups has been waged over the past three days. United Nations relief agency officials reported that over ten thousand Sudanese, many of them having to withstand blistering tropical heat of over 116 degrees, escaped the wrath of armed men who, in an offensive by loyalist forces, destroyed huts, burned crops, and shot men and women before shrinking back into the bush.

Facing a siege with artillery, rocket-powered grenades, and tank fire, civilians from rival ethnic groups attempted to defend their villages with outmoded weapons and spears. Scores of villagers put up a valiant fight against the insurgents, They took heavy casualties owing to the insurgent's superior firepower, before trying to escape with their families across the sand.

Witnesses said that at one point there was a standoff between the attackers and the civilians, as the male civilians shot the attackers and then retrieved their guns, turning them on the advancing group. However, eventually the tide turned, and the enemy lined up the civilian men, asked them if they would convert to Islam, and, when they refused, mowed them down with automatic weapons. Some of the elders were beheaded, and their heads displayed on top of wooden stakes.

A jihadist brigade captured a local hospital in the region, then paraded all the medical staff before a tribunal, quizzing them on their religious practices. One spokesman called their raid revenge for a Sudanese attack on several of their camps and pledged to retaliate against any troops and their supporters nearby. His group also said this was the beginning of an Islamic state in the southern part of Africa's most populous nation.

"We will punish the followers of Jesus Christ for their mission to colonize all the subjects within our borders," the spokesman said, noting that the government had been slow to respond. "We will punish them slowly and very cruelly."

UN spokesman Joseph Kagame confirmed the attack to the media.

The Sudanese army and local militias have signed alliances to penetrate the area under their control. The government has supplied several of the armed groups with automatic weapons, explosives, light artillery, and rocket-launched grenades. According to reports, villages were forcibly emptied and looted before being destroyed.

A witness in one of the remote villages said babies and small children were trampled in the exodus, with the sound of sporadic gunfire and shelling in the center of the structures. Fleeing in droves, the refugees sought protection at the UN camps some distance away. A number of refugees said they were scared to go back to their villages.

When UN peacekeepers arrived in two of the ravaged villages, they found hundreds of bodies in and around the huts, evidence of the uninterrupted violence that had taken place there.

"About two hundred fifty woman and children were rounded up and taken away to an undisclosed location," Kagame said. "After the attackers concluded their killing, the men of the village were given the order to convert. Those who refused were herded together at a school and shot at close range. Before their departure, the gunmen went from building to building, searching for anyone who was attempting to escape. The women and children were forcibly loaded onto buses and driven away. There is no protection for these people. The UN cannot stop the genocide. This part of Sudan stands at the precipice of disaster, as security is quickly deteriorating, signaling dire consequences for civilians and aid workers alike."

17

A NOTE ON SUFFERING

After two days on the front lines, I didn't know what to make of this Sudan madness, of what my eyes had seen, what my heart had witnessed, what my soul had experienced. This was beyond a struggle between good and evil. The sheer cruelty that this part of Africa was enduring went completely beyond a blood match between the believers of Allah and of Jesus Christ or the absurd cost of war.

Sweating like a pig in the tropics, I sat on my cot in one of the tents in the Doctors Without Borders camp, adjusted my mosquito net, and started contemplating what I would say in a letter to Owen, whose encouragement had brought us to this place. And before I lifted my pen, Elsa poked her head in the tent and yelled that she had a surprise for me tonight. I wondered what foolishness lay in store for me and how I could get out of anything that involved her. Addie was keeping a close eye on us. My assurances to her meant nothing.

Elsa was gone before I could say anything, so I went back to writing the letter. Hopefully, with no further interruptions, I could get this letter done, because I had no idea when I would get some downtime again.

Dear Owen:
Hope this letter finds you and your family well.
I've not been neglecting you, but idle time during

this Sudan adventure has been hard to come by. Every day has its share of events, both tragic and miraculous. This is the first time I've seen the agonies of war and destruction from a front-row seat, and I wonder how a soul can weather the hatred and malice it produces.

Shortly after my evening meal last night, I came across this verse from the apostle James. You may know it from Chapter four, Verse one: "From whence come war and fighting among you? Come they not hence, even of your lust that war in your members?"

As a messenger for Christ, I could dismiss this whole Sudan situation as a case of Christians being used as scapegoats again. I could yell for the civilized world not to turn its face and beseech it to acknowledge what is going on here. The amount of suffering and pain is enormous in this land. With constant distractions from other parts of the globe, our leaders, both political and spiritual, choose to show indifference and apathy when confronted with the fate of the Sudanese people, just like they did with the folks in Rwanda, Biafra, Uganda, and the Congo.

Because the world has been largely silent while these people have been slaughtered, I don't know how to process all this wholesale suffering done to the believers of our Lord. I don't want to come off like some ivory-tower academic, but our arrogance and insensitivity toward oppressed people cannot be excused in a heartbreaking case like this. Imagine the children of Ham turning a blind eye to this evil type of carnage. Dr. King taught us that all life is interrelated, but we have forgotten.

Yes, this world is something worse than I had expected or imagined. I cry for the humanity lost as the rape, torture, and killing continue. I watch the glory of evil at its peak. Its violations among believers and nonbelievers go unchecked, not just in its bizarre themes of religious persecution and tribal mayhem, but in its true contempt for life. These people are living for the moment. They are praying to survive one second to the next. They are trying to endure a life sentence of terror, suffering, and death.

Suffering, suffering, suffering. The news services are here, documenting the chaos, but take a photograph on any day and you'll see suffering on someone's face. The toll on innocent lives is mounting. Here is where dying a horrible death is a human experience that is more common than the joy of birth. As a witness of this disaster, I wonder, how do you escape the bloodlust and suffering? I have more questions than answers.

You cannot imagine the deep chill that penetrates you when you see bloated, rotten bodies in destroyed villages or along the roads. Life once filled this dead flesh. There were once human beings.

I'm questioning the works of God on earth now. This is something I never did before. I've become a questioning soul. Can the Lord turn His head when His people are suffering to this degree? How can these people hold fast to love and faith when despair and suffering surround them? How can you believe in a loving, caring God when hell is all around you?

Who speaks for these wretched, tormented people? Who talks for them in heaven? How can anything return to normal? I wonder about all these things. Like I said, I possess no answers, no solutions, no explanations, no understanding.

One of my professors in my seminary classes was fond of quoting from the bard William Shakespeare's The Tempest: *"Hell is empty. All the devils are here." In the Sudan, that is quite true.*

On this trip I feel like I'm swimming upstream. This bitter taste will not leave my mouth. I'm confused by all of this. Are humans this evil and violent? I believe in Christ. I can't blame or fault Him for all this suffering and pain. How can you be angry at life? But how can you draw back when the world becomes so cruel?

However, I understand that suffering in this life lasts only for a season. That's what I was trained to believe. That faith brought me through the tragedy with my late wife and the kids. It sustained me during some rough times with the rednecks in Alabama. I believe in the divine truth of God's supremacy in all things.

An aid worker, a Dinka man, said no one can see the face of the devil and live. Maybe that's true. Still, life is not that simple. I must get up off the floor, off my knees, and live. Make each day count.

Write back when you find a chance. Addie says hello.

Best, Clint

18

TAKING THE UNOFFICIAL TOUR

For the first time in Sudan, I suffered a bout of belly sickness, possibly from something I ate. Or drank. I spent the rest of the day nursing cramps and nausea and the ever-present runs. The doc gave me something for the symptoms, and by the start of the evening, I was feeling better. I gave the letter to Owen to the truck drivers to post. I lay there, listening to the roar of truck after truck bringing loads of refugees to the camps.

"Clint, the show's on!" Elsa exclaimed, squatting over me. "Come on. You can't miss this. You said you want to see things for yourself. Well, this is it! Now you'll see what everything is all about."

I sat up, my face a little green. "Can't you see that I'm sick?"

The journalist shook her head, taunting me. "Don't be a wimp. I'm tired of all your big talk. Go out on a limb for once and put your Christ to the test. He'll protect you. He's your lucky charm, right?"

If you wanted to provoke a Christian, all you had to do was have a nonbeliever ask you to put the Lord to the test. I knew what I had to do. I swung my legs over the edge of the cot, stretched my arms overhead, and asked Elsa to give me my pants. Compared to the refugees on the cots in the tents, I felt like a fraud, with only a slight fever, a sore throat, and a bellyache. These other folks were so much worse off; some were fighting for their lives due to malnutrition, dysentery, or gunshot wounds.

"I'll be back for you," Elsa said cheerily. "The truck will park out front. I'm taking just you. Addie doesn't want to go."

After she left, I put on my clothes, sprayed myself with bug spray, and placed two handkerchiefs in my pocket.

The sound of a horn interrupted any thoughts that I should be concerned or even alarmed about this next "adventure" with Elsa. I stepped out into the furnace, the oppressive heat of the African summer, immediately sweating beneath my shirt and pants. I hopped into the bed of the truck. In it were four armed men, two locals, and Elsa with her customary Nikon camera.

We drove off through the dark, our headlights providing the only illumination through the bush. I looked around at the blackness that had swallowed us up. Elsa was entertaining the men with flirtatious smiles, ribald talk, and humorous hand gestures. Two of the guys checked their weapons, making sure that they were properly loaded and would not jam when the moment happened.

Out of the darkness, a young girl ran toward the truck, her arms windmilling, her screams high-pitched. Elsa quieted instantly. The guns pointed at the panicked girl, who collapsed almost under the truck. One of the men in the truck jumped out and lifted her unconscious body. Her face was covered with deep cuts and bruises, her dress was torn, and blood was running down her thin black legs.

"Who would do this to her?" I asked aloud.

The others glanced at me and frowned. Everyone knew who had done this. After the man placed the girl gently in the truck and jumped in, we continued on for a short distance, until we could see the bright flashes of an inferno through the trees. We listened to the yells and screams coming from that direction, the pleas for help, the shrill sounds of loud whistles, and we smelled the acrid odor of wood burning. The truck pulled into a clearing, and we leaped from it to the hard ground. Elsa crouched down while the leader of this expedition told us not to bunch up, to keep low, and not to let them see us.

"We want to look, but we don't want to get involved," he explained. "If they see us, they will kill us. No doubt about that." He also warned us to watch out for land mines and booby traps. Sometimes the enemy set them around a camp to prevent villagers from escaping, thereby sealing them in and sending them to their doom.

While someone stayed with the injured girl, our group walked quietly through the trees, guided by the bright blaze and the gunfire. We moved from tree to tree, a few bullets whizzing by us in the air, cutting through the smoke.

"Keep down," the leader cautioned when another explosion shook the earth. Probably a mortar round.

Now we were close enough to see and hear the madness clearly—the enemy shooting every living thing, urgent shouts again, running between the huts. Some of the enemy troops threw grenades into some of the huts, sending people yelling and fleeing in all directions. The siege had begun in earnest. My face dripped with sweat. I could not stop my hands from trembling.

Who were these men and boys? Who were these killers and rapists? I tried to recall what the doctor had said. He'd said that these were members of the Bahr-el Ghazal tribes, the Binga, Banda, Shatt, Feroghe, Gula, and Kara. These were the names of the Islamic warriors fighting to create an *umma,* an Islamic community of believers.

The dead and the seriously wounded were sprawled out in the dirt. I watched as a man tried to run with his wife. Suddenly he stopped running, his legs gave out, and a single shot went through his body. He grabbed his chest with its large wound, vomited blood, and dropped sideways. The enemy seized his wife and put her among the women gathered at the entrance to the village. They burned the remainder of the huts, gathered the men and women whom they had not killed, and forced them to undress. The enemy didn't think they were evil; they were following the will of Allah and the holy teachings of the Koran. Their goal was to wipe out all followers of Christ and his infidel religion. Laughing and joking, the soldiers took turns shooting the villagers and smoking cigarettes.

Elsa's face was a picture of bliss and happiness. This was what she wanted to see. She aimed her camera at the atrocity, stopping only when the leader waved at her to put it down. She had only one master, the allure of media celebrity and a huge headline.

A group of soldiers ordered a young woman to dance for them. She knew it would be her last time, the last occasion when she would move her body to an earthly beat. The soldiers clapped in an odd rhythm while she attempted to sway. While the woman hopped and bounced, her fat breasts jiggled, and the men touched her rudely. In a split second she snatched a machete from one man and swung it at him, severing his head, sending it dropping to the ground. She stood there for two seconds. The soldiers shot her dead after that, the bullets slamming into her nude flesh. Then they led several men to the rear of the scorched huts and lined them up. The men offered no resistance and accepted their fate.

I prayed for them. A few wrung their hands and looked skyward as divine help was on the way. They dropped face-first when they were shot. Then one soldier walked among them and fired a single shot into their heads to insure they would not get up. Some soldiers hacked at their bodies, splattering blood all over their clothes.

One village elder was splashed with kerosene and torched. The old man ran in a mad circle, the flames climbing his body in yellow and orange plumes of heat. He made no sound. He didn't scream. Nobody went to help him. The soldiers laughed and pointed at his fatal jig.

A group of villagers fought back on the far side, shooting at the marauders. The enemy went crazy, opening fire wildly, sending bullets not only into the areas of the resistance but near us as well. There was no hiding place. Shots crashed into trees, snapping branches, spraying leaves. Gunfire followed those who ran through the darkness. They ran as fast as they could, not waiting for their death. I knelt silently in the bush, watching with the others as the massacre played itself out.

Some of the enemy sat in a circle, smoking cigarettes, while others forced themselves on the young girls and women. One or two of them stood in shadow against the smoking embers of the huts, allowing the adrenaline to subside, that biochemical rush that comes after a kill.

In the darkness, the leader of the militia split up the brigade, using smaller groups to search the huts and track down the villagers who were hiding or trying to escape. Sometimes there was a barrage of gunshots, usually automatic weapon fire, and then silence, and then the gunfire started up again. Before the soldiers departed, they stood and fired their weapons into the night sky to celebrate their victory.

A few villagers were able to hide until the violence stopped. We came out of hiding when we saw the enemy walk through the village, carrying their loot and leading the captive girls and women to their camp. Stumbling over bodies and blood trails, we ran toward the smoldering huts, hoping to rescue survivors. My pulse never slowed. I'd never felt fear like this. I knew my head had been in the crosshairs of some enemy rifle, but now I could relax. Dying so far away from home was not for me. "I can't believe this," I muttered.

With a sudden surge of energy, Elsa began snapping pictures of the survivors and the massacre. She found a boy, who collapsed in her arms, looking at her with impassive eyes, his head full of weeping sores and third-degree burns. I walked away from her and discovered a body that appeared to have been eaten by some animal. I couldn't tell if it was a man or a woman.

I walked through the demolished village in the direction of the truck. I kept rubbing my eyes. My legs pained me to no end. None of this made sense. My clothes were stiff with splattered blood and dirt. I leaned over and puked in the weeds and wiped my mouth. I had trouble catching my breath.

As I staggered to the truck, I saw two boys carrying their dead grandmother. I guessed they thought she was still breathing, but she was dead. Her eyes possessed that fatal sheen. Both boys were soaked with blood. Two of the men helped them onto the truck, while Elsa snapped pictures of the boys with their beloved corpse.

During the long ride back to the camp, nobody said a word. I couldn't help but think that all this suffering and death were calculated, planned carefully. How could the survivors forget or forgive this? And how could they heal if they could not forgive?

Nelson Mandela was right indeed. He knew suffering firsthand.

19

SUDAN PROPER

Upon my return to the camp late that night, I felt emotionally drained from the tragedy I had just witnessed. I made my way to my tent and plopped down on my cot. I couldn't sleep. Hours later, I waved away Elsa when she peeked her head in the tent. She wanted to talk about the massacre, but I needed time to process the wanton killing and rape. I was still in shock from what I had seen. She muttered under her breath and left in a huff. No sooner had I closed my eyes than I felt a finger poke me on the cheek.

"Can I see you outside, Clint?" It was Addie, giving me the evil eye. "It won't take long. I promise."

It was still dark. Morning had not arrived yet.

"Okay, okay." I rose and followed her outside.

Out in the yard, we leaned on one of the trucks and talked. She looked me up and down with a piercing glance. The woman wore the same clothes she had had on yesterday. Possibly, she had not slept at all. Her fatigue showed around her eyes and mouth.

Addie was the first to speak. "I saw you leave with Elsa. Where did you guys go? You seemed to be in a hurry."

I frowned and tried to ignore her. "Addie, you called me out here for this? I don't get you. You're imagining things."

"I saw you with my own eyes," she insisted.

"You probably did." I was getting mad.

"So where did you go?" She was not going to let me get off easy.

I looked at her with a bored expression. "I'm tired, Adele. I had a rough day. Maybe I'll tell you about it later."

"Why can't you tell me about it now?"

I didn't speak. I started to walk back to the tent.

Addie grabbed me by the arm. "Clint, I don't even know how old you are. I know so little about you. You tell me so little."

"Why is that important?" I asked.

"It just is," she replied. "I want to know how old you are."

I removed her hand. "What difference does that make?"

"Sometimes you seem very immature for a man your age," she said, pouting. "You act like a teenager with your hormones acting up. You don't act like a man."

"What?" I was surprised by her response.

Addie folded her arms and spoke to me like the teacher she was. "You act like you're going through puberty. You keep secrets."

"Is this about Elsa again?" I replied. "Sometimes you get on my nerves."

She was fuming, angry that her tactics were not drawing me out. "You're a liar. A big liar. Like most men, you think lying is very natural. You don't know how to tell the truth."

I repeated the question. "Is this about Elsa again? I told you that you were jealous of her. You measure yourself against her."

"That's crap." She was really upset.

"No, it's not." I didn't know why I was putting up with her foolishness. I think I was still dazed from all the scenes of suffering and death I'd witnessed hours earlier. I wondered how cops and soldiers could deal with a steady diet of this kind of horror.

"Clint, I'm not studying her," she said harshly. "She's a loose woman. I told you this."

Just then, three guys with guns walked past, their weapons held low, on a patrol. We stopped talking until they had gone on.

"I don't care what Elsa does," I said. "My only concern is getting out of this hellhole alive. These people on both sides are out of their minds. The only thing they worship is death."

She noticed something in my face. I could never fool her.

"What's the matter?" she asked.

"Oh, nothing."

"You saw something that upset you. Out there. What did you see?"

I wasn't going to talk about it, not tonight. "Nothing."

Her eyes searched my expression for any clues. "You look a bit different. You look like you saw something out there."

I looked off into the night sky, in search of the coming sunrise. "Addie, I never understood what evil was until I came to this place. I thought some of the craziness in Harlem was over the top. Not so. That's the Little League compared to the work of the demons here."

She laughed bitterly. "Harlem or Sudan. Take your choice."

I watched the men on patrol take up their posts at the checkpoint. "Right. It's not necessary to choose. Sudan is out in front. Sudan wins hands down."

She listened to me ranting and drew a different conclusion. "Were you this talkative with your late wife? It's very hard to get anything out of you."

"I haven't changed," I said, disagreeing with her. "I think we talked about things that mattered. If it didn't matter, then we kept our mouths closed and said nothing. Terry liked that about me."

Her wry smile denied the truth of what I was saying. "Clint, you're fooling yourself. I tell you, you're cold. Your wife killed off all your emotions. I need more. I want more. I want more from my man."

"Am I your man, Addie?"

She didn't miss a beat. "Yes, but I just want things to be different. This place has changed you. Maybe it's changed both of us."

I agreed. "Absolutely."

"Clint, what did you see?" she asked again.

"Nothing."

Addie was furious. "You're like Elsa, who sees me as a country hick. You pay me no mind. Other men like me. I could get anybody around here to pay me some attention. I'm not a party girl. I'm particular about what I do with men."

"For how long?" I replied. "You're flirting, just like Elsa."

"Are you trying to hurt me?" Her eyes were flashing with temper.

"No."

She glared at me intensely. "I don't follow you. Why are you trying to insult me?"

"I'm not," I said, denying her accusation.

"Clint, then why did you say that mess? Why?"

I turned the focus around to her, making her look at herself.

"Addie, I see major changes in your behavior," I said. "Suddenly, you smoke like a fiend and drink liquor. This is something you didn't do before. Every time I see you, you got a gang of men leering at you like you're fresh meat. And you flirt with them like crazy."

"Is that how you describe me?" she asked.

"Yes. A tart."

"A what?" she asked. This was news to her.

"You bet." I wanted her to see herself realistically.

"Maybe I just want attention," she replied. "Every woman wants to get attention. No female wants to be ignored. That's human nature."

Now it was time to get her to realize that Elsa was a woman as well. And human. "Does that include Elsa?" I asked. "Maybe that's why she's acting like she does."

She didn't want to hear any of that. "We're not talking about Elsa. We're talking about me. Me."

I flashed her my best outlaw smile. "I'm saying that's why Elsa is so popular. I don't know her that well. But I bet she's craving attention as well."

"Elsa's not so saintly, so innocent," she said. "She's giving the boys what they want."

"Does that include me, Addie?"

"Maybe," she answered. "You won't tell me where you went with her last night. You won't tell me that."

"You're right," I said, strengthening my resolve. "We have discussed Elsa and her behavior before. Tell me this. Are you in a competition with her? Tell me the truth."

"Heck no!"

I recalled Terry, another woman who was important to my life. "Like my late wife, Elsa likes men. Terry was the same way. They get a thrill being around so much beefcake."

Addie refused to acknowledge that she and Elsa were similar in this way. "I'm not like her."

"I think it's normal for women to compete with each other," I replied. "It's healthy. Men do it all the time."

"That's stupid," she declared.

"Adele, I wonder why you came here, when you're not the least political," I countered. "When the doctors and the staff discuss the state of affairs, what's going on here, you say nothing. You sit there like a log. Even the drivers contribute to the conversation."

She turned her back to me. "I don't have to run my mouth like some people. You always have to be the center of attention. You're a show-off."

"Is that what you think of me? I'm just a curious fellow."

Imitating a small child, she whined, "Why? Why? Why?"

I grinned. "Now you're mocking me. Why are you so angry with me? What is it that you expect me to do?"

"Be yourself," she retorted. "I know that's hard for you. I no longer know who you are. Who are you?"

"I am me," I said firmly.

She disagreed with me strongly. "That's not true. You do everything to not be yourself. You're a phony. I bet you even lie to yourself when you're alone."

I looked deeply into her eyes. "I made a choice to follow you. I wanted you in my life, but now I'm not so sure."

"Why is that, Clint?" she asked. "Is it because I'm asking you all these questions? I'm interested. I want to know you."

"Love is not easy," I said. "After what I've been through, who can I trust? I don't want a repeat of what happened to me with Terry. I want someone who can bring out the best in me."

"Can you give me the benefit of the doubt?"

"I don't know."

She winked at me seductively. "Maybe I can become the person you want to love. I know God ain't finished with me yet."

"I'm a work in progress as well," I said, snickering.

"I was trying to figure out why I am so attracted to you," she said. "You are a real mystery. I love a man, a preacher with a strange past."

"A strange past?"

"Yes, your story fascinated me to no end," she said.

I laughed again. "I guess I just want to stay on top of my feelings. I don't want them to control me. Maybe that's why I'm here. I want to learn about myself. I want to rejoin life."

She brushed her khaki shorts off. "All I ask is that you talk to me, tell me the truth, and not tell me what you think I want to hear. Is that all right with you?"

"Yes," I replied.

"Clint, you won't believe this," she said curiously. "Africa is really having an effect on me. I should have had my period already, but I haven't had one since I got here. I spot sometimes and get cramping. But no period."

"It's too early for menopause," I joked.

"I know, but it concerns me," she said. "I'm going to talk to the doctor about it. I hope nothing is wrong with me. I know I'm not pregnant. I haven't done anything."

I started laughing and couldn't stop. "Addie, is my hour up? Can I get your permission to leave and wring out a kidney? Mother, may I?"

Before she could reply, I went into the shadows, to the latrine.

20

REVERENCE

It happened that next Wednesday I finally got a tour of the Doctors Without Borders camp, with Dr. Arriale serving as a guide. He took me through a collection of tents and around the expanse of ground that held the crowded refugee quarters. The tall doctor apologized for having neglected me, but he had a good reason to do so, and that was that the camp had accepted another band of people fleeing for their lives. They had traveled for many miles, dodging enemy militias, trying to sustain their existence without food and water.

"We're seeing more new arrivals, much more than this camp can accommodate," Dr. Arriale said while he showed me the perimeter. "I wonder whether we can continue to deliver essential humanitarian aid services. It's not about donations or staffing, but about the massive amount of supplies needed."

I stepped up my pace to match his long, loping gait. "I have watched them come to the camp, and most of them are in really bad shape. They're weak, hungry, very sickly."

We stood and watched three trucks in the distance pull up to a series of tents that were segregated from the others. Workers, dressed in strange medical suits, carried fragile refugees off the trucks and took them inside the tents, handling them gingerly, careful not to bounce their skeletal frames.

The doctor smirked and shook his head. "The increase in refugees is taking up so much room outside this original camp, stretching the limits of the security we can provide them. We'd love to send them home, but the violence is still raging there."

I asked the question that most of us wanted to ask but were afraid to do so. "What is going on over there, in those tents? The staff won't let us go near there."

"It's cholera, Reverend," the doctor said sadly.

Science had not been my favorite subject in school. I did horribly in biology and chemistry; in fact, I almost failed those courses. Karen, a high school friend, had tutored me, and I'd got passing grades. She later died in a hit-and-run near her home, the victim of a drunk driver.

"What's cholera?" I asked innocently. "It's not like the Ebola virus, right?"

Dr. Arriale started to walk toward the tents, gesturing with his hands as he moved through a small group of refugees who were staring at the bush, wishing they could go home.

"Cholera is an acute bacterial infection in the intestines," he explained. "It's spread in unsanitary, crowded conditions. Usually, the infected person has intense bouts of diarrhea and vomiting, leading to critical dehydration and death. This is a very painful disease."

I halted in my tracks. "Can it be cured?"

The doctor smiled knowingly, then said that it could be cured.

"You've got to get the patient treated early," he told me. "It can be effectively treated if treatment is started as soon as the person presents with any symptoms. We replace the lost fluid and electrolytes, such as sodium and potassium, with an oral rehydration solution. Sometimes we have to do this intravenously with the more severe cases."

"How many cholera cases do you have in this camp?"

The doctor noted that since the government's ministry of health had officially recorded an outbreak in this area, they had tallied over two thousand cases, and more suspected cases were awaiting lab confirmation. He said he had got funds to open a cholera treatment center, which would offer safe water and the cholera vaccine to the camp.

"We had eight hundred cholera patients up until the rainy season, and then the numbers skyrocketed," the doctor said. "I know a few people at Doctors Without Borders in Juba, and they provided more beds, testing kits, chlorine solution, and rehydration salts. That gave us a leg up on this epidemic."

I mentioned the bodies I'd seen being carried out of the tents, wrapped in plastic and sealed, then loaded onto trucks. The doctor would not acknowledge that these were the ones whom treatment could not cure.

"What do you do with the dead?" I asked.

The doctor didn't reply. He switched topics and spoke about a massive cholera vaccination effort in the camp. Some refugees needed two rounds of the vaccine to avoid infection. The staff followed up on the required inoculations, but sometimes even those who had had the pair of shots contracted the horrific disease.

We stepped into a tent where the staff treated war wounds, gunshot wounds, serious burns, and amputations. There were forty beds in the large tent. The patients, mostly women and children, kept the nurses and attendants hopping. They administered painkillers, adjusted bandaged stumps, and performed many other tasks.

"I came here from the Bentiu Hospital a few months ago," Dr. Arriale said, noticing my bewildered gaze. "We had a street battle in town, and the violence spilled over into the hospital. Hospitals are supposed to be places of comfort and safety. Not true in this case. Over thirty-three people were killed by the militia at the hospital."

I took a deep breath and said, "No reasonable person would kill the sick," but then I remember the other night.

"Hospitals in South Sudan are often under attack," the doctor said. "The patients were killed randomly. However, some of those who had fled to the hospital were targeted because they were from a different tribe or religion. Twenty-one people were marched from the facility and murdered behind the building."

"Evil reigns in this place," I said somberly.

"The violence here is very brutal and cruel," the doctor observed. He paused when one of the nurses asked him to sign a prescription. "The enemy fighters searched for boys and men who had left their ranks and refused to kill anymore. They shot them dead where they stood. When I left to go home, the streets were littered with dead civilians. My place was ransacked, so I fled to the United Nations mission, and from there, I came here."

"How can you bear it?" I asked. "How can anybody bear this misery?"

He stopped near the bed of a man wrapped in bandages from head to chest, and stuck a thermometer into the hole for his mouth. The patient lay quietly, moving his head only.

"He's a burn victim," the doctor said. "We found him among the people outside the camp. He was in dire need of assistance. The others did what they could for him, but they notified us when his condition became worse. We've done all we can for him. We make him comfortable with painkillers."

He walked along the row of beds, stopping occasionally to chat with this one and that one. A nurse followed him, taking notes about meds and their schedule. His manner was friendly, never patronizing. The place smelled of bleach, alcohol, sweat, burnt flesh, and decay.

"We can't let the refugees stay here forever," he said. "We have a backlog of them. We have no screening center at the camp. We try to register them so they can get needed items, such as blankets, cooking utensils, soap, and such. The government allows us to truck water to temporary silos. CARE, the Red Cross, Oxfam, and some of the faith-based organizations and charities have really come through for us in our time of need."

"I've heard that some of the girls and women have been molested in the camp," I said, hoisting an eyebrow. "Can you provide protection to them while they're in your care?"

"No, we cannot," he insisted. "We're worried about the enemy militias and their raids. If a woman feels threatened, she can report the situation to us, and we'll provide security. But there are too many cases here."

"I feel badly for the girls and women here," I murmured.

The doctor did his rounds, preparing his patients for treatment, putting on a good face for both those who were recovering and the critically ill. He told me that too many people were dying from preventable diseases because of the horrible conditions in the camps. He was ashamed of this fact.

I remained silent. *War, famine, disease. Simply hell.*

"What complicated our cholera crisis was the latrines overflowing and contaminating our water," the doctor said mournfully. "We're trying to make sure that problem doesn't happen anymore. Our funding is stable, but we don't plan ahead. We might have a shortfall."

"And the government doesn't help matters?" I asked him.

The doctor said no. "The government is concerned only about the oil profits. Oil is king. Oil makes up ninety-eight percent of Sudan's budget. The real reason for all this turmoil is not religion but economics. About seventy-five percent of the oil lies in the south, but all the pipelines flow north. Khartoum gets all of the profits. You figure it out."

"Most Americans believe the war in Iraq was started for oil," I said. "In fact, Bush lied to us when he said we had to fight the Iraqis because they possessed biological weapons. Inspectors searched, but no such weapons were found."

"Exactly," the doctor agreed. "That's the situation here too."

"Will the administrators expand this camp?" I asked.

"I don't know," he replied. "There are certain government restrictions that prevent new humanitarian workers from accessing specific regions. It doesn't matter how many people have been displaced by the conflict. Nobody talks about this. But the government can't even provide basic services for its own people."

"Why doesn't the world call attention to all this baloney?"

The doctor stuck his gloved hands in his pockets, suddenly very angry. "The European Union has imposed sanctions on the government's military leaders. They imposed travel bans and asset freezes on some of the army heads, but that doesn't do anything. They laugh at the sanctions. The government keeps supplying arms to the various militias and violating the cease-fire agreements. And the killings and rapes go on."

"Elsa gave me the history of the truces and cease-fires, and they have flopped repeatedly," I said. "I can't believe this."

The doctor chuckled. "I like that Elsa. Interesting woman."

"Isn't there an arms embargo against Sudan?" I said, not wanting to talk about the perturbing British journalist.

"Yes, there is, Reverend."

"Are you serving displaced persons in remote areas other than this region?" I asked him while he put a stethoscope to a boy's chest.

"Oh yes, there is funding, but we don't know how reliable it is," the doctor answered. "Plans for several camps in areas along the border are in the works. Also, we need more doctors and nurses to staff the camps. Recruitment is key."

Suddenly, Dr. Bromberg, with three medical attendants at his side, trotted across the room, waving frantically. He yelled that two more trucks full of critical cholera patients had arrived. "All hands on deck," he called.

"Someone once said, 'Why would we want to help people in a faraway country with an unpronounceable name?'" my doctor guide said, moving toward Dr. Bromberg and the attendants. "Is this crazy, Reverend?"

We walked out of the tent and into the glaring sun, then watched the old routine: staffers unloading the sick to transport them into the tent. One of the staffers commented, "The parade never stops, never lets up."

21

LIES TO TELL CHRISTIANS

The camp was buzzing with the news about the negotiations in Addis Ababa, Ethiopia, between representatives of the Sudanese government and the Sudanese Peoples Liberation Movement. It was the seventh round of talks with a series of postponements. Their concentration was the fighting in South Kordofan and Blue Nile, two southern states along the border with South Sudan. I read the newspaper with my interview about the massacre in one of those border regions.

One of the witnesses to the recent mass killing in a small village in Sudan, Reverend Clint Winwood, a prominent New York City minister, spoke to a reporter for the Daily Telegraph *about the atrocities. He is currently on a fact-finding mission through the region, documenting instances of religious persecution and ethnic cleansing. Articulate and devout, the minister has called on the world to bring a halt to the genocide occurring in South Sudan and Darfur.*

Colin Samet: How long have you been in the country?

Reverend Winwood: I've been here in Sudan for about three weeks.

Samet: Have you had any trouble with the Sudanese government?

Reverend Winwood: No more than usual. I was warned not to go into this area, because they said the government could not be responsible for my safety. I've seen my share of suffering and misery.

Samet: Do you hold the government responsible for the murders, rapes, and looting you've seen? Are they supplying the militias who are responsible for these unlawful acts?

Reverend Winwood: Back in twenty eleven, Sudanese president Omar al-Bashir told reporters that the government had decided that Sudan would have a strict Islamic identity. This year government officials were on hand to witness the demolition of a Christian church, saying they needed the land to build affordable housing. Also, they decreed that there would be a ban on future church construction. They said they had enough Christian churches in the country.

Samet: Do you believe them?

Reverend Winwood: No, I don't. There should be religious liberty.

Samet: Have you seen persecution in action?

Reverend Winwood: Yes, I have. Still, I only hope the country's opposing forces can come together and stop fighting. We need a lasting peace. The people in this country need a permanent peace and a halt to the violence.

Samet: How will they do that? Cease-fires and truces have been signed and later violated. There were peace talks in Addis Ababa, but nothing has come of it. In fact, some say the violence has escalated.

Reverend Winwood: Maybe the European Union and the United States need to really step in and negotiate the peace. I'm surprised that the Arab League or some reputable Arab organization has not brokered some sort of settlement.

Samet: How do you feel President Obama has done in terms of the Sudanese crisis?

Reverend Winwood: The president has his plate full, putting out fires all over the world. America is war weary. I'm also surprised that more African American churches are not involved in ending the Sudanese crisis. They seem to be more involved in this gospel of prosperity and profit than in African politics and the plight of Christians worldwide.

Samet: What did you see the other night, during the massacre in that small, remote village in Sudan?

Reverend Winwood: I saw an attack by one of the militias on a small village, where the soldiers went from house to house, searching for Christians and other people who aren't loyal to their cause. The men were rounded up and shot. The soldiers took some of the girls and women hostage. Who knows their fate? Someone said they will be sold or given to members of the militias as sex slaves.

Samet: Did you see instances of assault and rape?

Reverend Winwood: Yes, I did.

Samet: Could you and the others give any assistance?

Reverend Winwood: No, we could not. We were outnumbered and outgunned. It was one of the most terrible experiences in my life.

Samet: Switching gears, what are your duties at the refugee camp there? Are you rolling up your sleeves?

Reverend Winwood: I do what I can. My first responsibility is to serve God and to minister to the people. At the camp, I've visited the sick, ministered to the critically ill and wounded, and performed funerals. As a Christian pastor, I try to show myself as an example worthy of dignity and respect. I send a message to these poor, displaced souls that all men and women are the children of God. I practice a gospel of love and hope in some evil times. Sudan is ripe for salvation.

Samet: Some say the battle in Sudan, along with other parts of the Middle East and Africa, is economic, not Christian versus Islam. You touched on this earlier, but you didn't elaborate on it.

Reverend Winwood: I forget who, but someone once said, "One cannot minister to the soul and ignore either the health of the body or the effects and relations of the social environment." That is the role of the Christian church. The church has to free Africans from the shackles of magic and myth.

Samet: How can the church achieve this goal when it is operating in a heated climate of violence, killings, and genocide?

Reverend Winwood: I agree. This is a tough nut to crack. Genocide is not about minor frustrations, annoyances, and petty slights. Some of these conflicts have been going on for generations and generations. Some of them are tribal, and some of them are religious. Some of these wars and struggles are the aftermath of colonialism. But as some of the Christian ministers who I admire tremendously said the other day, we are our brother's keeper and we will not submit to evil forces, no matter how overwhelming or powerful.

Samet: That's almost romantic. But how do you give the more than half a million refugees in Sudan the strength to sustain their faith when everything seems to go against them?

Reverend Winwood: Going back to my original message, we must provide for their basic human needs in order for the people to sustain their faith. We must help them keep their faith alive. Reading the Bible and being baptized are not enough to help them survive. This is hard work. That's why I love the faith-based organizations and charities. They are taking up the slack for the UN, CARE, and the Red Cross. They are making a difference.

Samet: This seems to be a highly personal cause for you. Why is that so? Why do you need to be here at this time?

Reverend Winwood: This is a spiritual pilgrimage for me in a way. I'm saying to the Lord, "Here I stand. Use me." After a time of prayer and talks with some leading church officials in the States and here in the region, I realized that I must speak out. It was not a difficult choice. This journey has totally changed my worldview.

Samet: What do you mean, Reverend?

Reverend Winwood: I've weathered some great challenges in life, several tragedies, but nothing compares to those faced by these Sudanese refugees. This trip has totally changed my perspective on life. Back in the States, after I went through a very life-altering experience, I was bitter, angry, isolated. Maybe I became self-important and arrogant. Some of the church officials said I'd lost the common touch. I was removed from the things that brought me pleasure and joy, that brought me a sense of satisfaction in working with the community. I stepped away from the church. My ministry ceased to be about Sundays, the mother board, the choir, or sermons. That is, until I went South to assist a friend. Alabama, that is. Everything changed. I gradually came back to the land of the living.

Samet: In your opinion, what do the Sudanese people want other than religion? Is that all they want?

Reverend Winwood: Are you crazy? They want a decent life. They want a life like we have, to enjoy their families, to have good shelter, to watch their children grow up. They want the life they see portrayed by the media in the West, where religious freedom can be celebrated. All they want, all any of them wants, is to be blessed with opportunity and hope.

Samet: What is keeping them from reaching their goal?

Reverend Winwood: The government in the north, I think.

Samet: Explain, please.

Reverend Winwood: Don't play coy. Look around you. The government has an agenda to displace the civilians in Darfur and in the south because of oil, not religion. We touched on this before. That is why they have targeted certain groups. The government does not protect these people. No peace deal is stable.

Samet: At the peace talks, I understand the government stated that it does not want to have a peacekeeping force in the southern part of Sudan. All sides have been slow to act on this. The killing and famine continue. Peacekeepers would cut down on some of the violence we see in the region. Why has the peacekeeping force been rejected?

Reverend Winwood: One of the aid doctors said that China has made a big, multibillion-dollar investment in the Sudanese oil fields. Some say over eight billion dollars. In the UN, China blocks anything being done about the killings and the genocide. The oil fields are in the south, but all the pipelines flow north. It seems many of the superpowers want to get in the game.

Samet: You brought up the religious angle. That cannot be ignored. First, do you consider yourself a deeply religious person?

Reverend Winwood: Yes, I do.

Samet: Do you believe that God is a product of the human imagination? Do you believe humans could make up a belief system that could get them off the hook in terms of ethics and behavior?

Reverend Winwood: Look around you at the wonders of life. Do you think this is a hologram? Do you think this is a dream? I don't think so.

Samet: You have different faiths competing for dominance in the world. It's like the War of the Roses or the Crusades. The fact of the matter is that human beings are fighting over their concept of God and faith. Can you accept that? China has nothing to do with this.

Reverend Winwood: God, Allah, Yahweh, or whatever. Yes, we have different views of God and faith, but there's a similarity between them when you melt them down. As for the battle between faiths, who knows what God thinks? Who can speak for God? It's a problem for me when humans speak for God with so much confidence. I've read a few articles recently that said that religious persecution is not a big issue today, and that is just not true. It's not just in the schoolbooks. It's here, it's now, and more than a billion people cannot worship the way they want.

Samet: Intolerance is very much with us.

Reverend Winwood: Blasphemy laws exist in several Arab nations. Ancient Christian communities suffer persecution every day. Some sources say that over one hundred fifty thousand Christians are killed each year because they worship the Lord.

Samet: For example, the Western media has spotlighted Boko Haram, an extremist Muslim group that has attacked Christians and Muslims alike in Nigeria. The group kidnapped the girls and women in several villages and held them for ransom. Some of them were sold as sex slaves, and others just vanished. Who knows what happened to them?

Reverend Winwood: I have read about their plight. But you must know that Christians are the most persecuted all over the world. Everybody hates us. That's why we must campaign for religious freedom. It is a building block for most of the other freedoms. Usually when you have religious liberty, you have freedom of the press, freedom of assembly, freedom to vote, freedom to learn. However, many countries of the world are afraid to let their citizens worship their own God in their own way. And that's why we had the ethnic killings in Bosnia, Germany, the Middle East, and now Sudan. Violence, death, repression.

Samet: Sudan, which is largely Muslim in the north, has been in a struggle with its Christian population for more than forty years. It's Africa's longest civil war. In reality, it has had two civil wars since 1955. The conflict heated up when South Sudan became an independent country in twenty eleven. Christians in the northern part of Sudan are having a very difficult time at present.

Reverend Winwood: In America we don't have the truly horrific images of Sudan or any of the other trouble spots in Africa. Images of a starving child, a row of burning huts, or a destroyed church will be carried on the TV evening news, but our news is sanitized. But I am on the ground, witnessing the beheadings, the machete-hacked limbs, the girls and women raped, the entire families wiped out. It is appalling.

Samet: Does the fact that President Obama has not acknowledged that America is a Judeo-Christian nation factor into Sudan's turmoil?

Reverend Winwood: The president of the United States is not the president of the world. He has very little influence over what is done in Africa. America has very little wiggle room in deciding the affairs of Africa. We threw that advantage away when we went into Iraq after the nine-eleven tragedy. Bush lied, Cheney lied, and Powell lied.

Samet: Are you saying that Islam is the enemy? Are you saying the Muslims are the cancer of the civilized world?

Reverend Winwood: You keep trying to put words in my mouth. Islam is not the enemy and never has been. There are fine and upstanding worshippers of the Islamic faith. They do not use the Koran as a license to slaughter other human beings. I was on a panel with two Muslim clerics, and they were as appalled as I was with the extremist actions in the Middle East and Central Africa.

Samet: But you must say there has been a lot of violence and death connected to the extremist Islamic followers. Every day you see killings and bombings involving members of that faith. Explain that.

Reverend Winwood: Again, Islam is not the enemy. I recall a statement by a group of one hundred thirty-eight Muslim clerics that was sent to Christian leaders in two thousand seven and that called for peace and understanding between the two religions. The clerics wrote, "If Muslims and Christians are not at peace, the world cannot be at peace." In their statement they asked for respect, fair play, kindness, compassion, and a life filled with peace, harmony, and mutual goodwill.

Samet: Then why can't these leading Muslim clerics exert some influence to stop the killings?

Reverend Winwood: I don't know. That mystifies me.

Samet: Are you afraid that this interview will get you in trouble with the government of Sudan? Just like the North Korean government, the Sudanese government is keeping a close eye on all foreigners, especially Christian leaders. No doubt they have an eye on you.

Reverend Winwood: I don't worry about that. I'm here doing the Lord's will, and nothing will stop me from doing that.

22

BACK TO THE ACTION

Three days after the newspaper article was published, Elsa suddenly appeared while I walked through the tents to the loading area. The heat was sapping all the energy of the foreigners, who seemed to sag in their sweat-drenched clothes under the searing summer sun. Nevertheless, Elsa looked refreshed and eager to chat. I was trying to make it from point A to point B, as I wanted to discuss with someone how I could get a ride to Juba, the capital of South Sudan. There was a fully operational airport from Juba. I was thinking of throwing in the towel.

"Read your interview, Reverend," Elsa chirped. "So you use your head for more than a hat rack. I didn't know you're on top of the things here. They'll be talking about your interview all over."

I wiped my forehead, mumbling. "I didn't do it to get publicity. I hoped only to get some of my opinions across to the African spiritual community. I'm not a tourist here."

She laughed out loud. "Good for you. Reverend, you tell them what you think. However, it might get you into trouble with Khartoum. They don't like to be double-crossed. They figure they gave you free rein, and you do something like this interview."

"Khartoum can take a flying leap," I growled. "I just wanted to get on the record about how I felt about this madness. The government has declared war on the Christian community, and I don't like it."

Elsa became stern and irritated. "Reverend, you're going to make it very tough for us in the media to get access to the government for our stories. Some of the guys, especially the folks at Reuters and the *Guardian,* were barking at me because I brought you with me. The security forces have already contacted us to lodge a complaint."

"Nobody has called me or contacted me," I admitted.

Elsa grinned. "And they wouldn't. They think we can keep you on a short leash. They told us that we were responsible for you."

"I didn't know that," I said, moving into the shade.

"Also, did you know that Addie has been playing cozy with this big Dinka guard," she said. "She should be careful with him. We think this guy plays for the other team, the government. The doctors and the staff steer clear of him."

I thought for a moment. *What can a naive country girl do to ruin herself in a strange land with a double agent who would kiss her rather than kill her?* Maybe she was thinking she was getting back at me. Maybe she was imagining that Elsa and I had a hot thing going, and she was trying to protect herself.

"That's nuts," I said. "I should warn her."

Elsa was adamant in her opinion. "Don't. Let her grow up. She feels she's above all this. She needs to get her feet wet. I don't like her. She's a real phony. She loves everybody."

"I don't know what she's trying to prove," I said.

"When we came back from the massacre, I saw her drinking with the guys, chugging the stuff," she said. "She was pals with everyone. They treated her like one of the guys. And then she went off with this big native, who, I know, means her no good."

I didn't know what to make of this new Addie. "I've got to warn her. She could really get hurt. She doesn't know the rules in this game."

"The Africans think she's easy, because she lacks formality," she added. "They like rules and regulations. A little distance. That is when they are at their best. She's easy and loose. She's hugging everybody as the men smell the liquor on her breath. I tried to say something to her, and she got real snippy."

"The other night she couldn't look me in the eye," I said. "She thinks we're an item. I told her no. Everything's sex with her lately."

"Reverend, have you slept with her?"

I shook my head. "No."

"Are you serious about her?" she asked.

"I was, but I've had to rethink that," I confessed. "She's very confused. She doesn't know what she wants. I think she's depressed. Sometimes when a woman is the saddest, there can be trouble."

"That's why you need to let her alone," she said firmly. "Let her learn for herself. Don't act like her father. She needs a man, not a daddy."

"We'll see, Elsa," I said. "Still, I'm worried about her."

Elsa suddenly brightened up, her voice hitting new high notes. "Guess what? One of the warlords, one of the guys who directed the raid on the village the other night, turned himself in to the authorities. He had one of his representatives try to negotiate a deal of safe passage with the Americans. The Yanks said, 'No dice.' They said they are going to turn him over to the International Criminal Court so it can charge him with crimes against humanity."

"Oh, man, I prayed for him," I said. "I think I saw him, the one with the thick arms and the red scarf. He had two automatics tucked in his waist."

"That was him," she said.

"That's great news," I said. "How are the locals responding?"

Elsa smiled slyly. "The people in the camps, the human rights groups, the spiritual community, and the UN are loving it. They're cheering the move. This is one bad guy out of the way."

"Do you feel safe here?" I asked her, looking at the barbed-wire perimeter ringing the camp.

"It's as safe as any camp along the border," she replied.

"Did you know we have a cholera epidemic in the camp, Elsa?" I asked. "Dr. Arriale says the refugees are infected with an unusual cholera strain. He didn't want to tell me about the outbreak."

Elsa shrugged. "He told me too. He says it got into the water supply and was hard to contain. Over three hundred people have died so far, and about fifteen hundred have been infected with this bug."

"It's a horrible death," I told her. "I've seen it."

Elsa nudged me in the arm and whispered, "These are not the cleanest people on the planet. If they would wash their hands after they squatted in the bush or in the water, cholera would vanish overnight. You know it's true, Reverend."

"Elsa, you sound like some of these white folks around here who think all Africans are savages," I said curtly. "Some of the disasters that have befallen them are not their doing. The doctor was telling me about Haiti's cholera epidemic that started in two thousand ten, after the earthquake. It was brought to the island by Nepalese peacekeepers who were based by a river. It killed over eighty-five hundred locals, and more than seven hundred thousand were infected. I think this is the case here."

"Huh? There are no Nepalese troops here."

I stared at her. "The doctors told me that the cholera outbreak worsened during the rainy season, when water got into the latrines and the bad bacteria overflowed into the water supply. Before that, there was only a small number of cases."

"I don't believe that," Elsa said.

"Dr. Bromberg said lab tests confirmed that only two people living in another section of the camp have cholera, but he fears the disease will spread rapidly because of the poor living conditions," I explained. "Other than washing hands, he wanted water shipments chlorinated to kill cholera bacteria."

"How many people are they seeing in the other area of the camp?"

"Elsa, the staff says they're seeing forty patients," I said. "Dr. Bromberg said he has put in for more supplies, including doses of vaccine, water pumps, mobile latrines, and water purification tablets. The staff has started a cholera elimination campaign, promoting boiling water for at least ten minutes before drinking it or cooking with it."

"Reverend, that's not going to help," Elsa said snidely. "They are filthy people, and they are living in filthy conditions. They are so hungry that they can barely eat. The food given to some of them is killing them, because their bodies cannot stand the shock. These people are some of the refugees who were starving and ate leaves. It's not going to help. If you get water, you drink, period."

"You sound so negative," I told her.

"There is no hope here," she replied. "Just like in Rwanda, Biafra, the Congo, and Angola. Africans love to suffer. They simply love it. Ever been to the other side of the camp, with its all dirt, filth, and tiny makeshift tents? A large number of the people there are sleeping on the ground. I bet the doctors haven't taken you there. They don't want you to see it."

Just then, a supply truck rumbled up, dust flying up to engulf it, and parked before the garage. We looked on as two Dinka guards dragged a body, the head thrown back and the arms dangling at its sides. I stepped away from Elsa to get a closer look. The guards held up a drunk Addie, her front covered with puke, her legs dragging on the ground like those of a rag doll.

"That's the fellow there, the dark purple one," Elsa said. "Seems like she had herself a time. A grand old time."

We watched them struggle to get Addie up the steps, one at a time. She was not a lightweight. If I knew anything about drunken people who had passed out, it was that they usually were not as light as a feather. I broke away from the reporter and followed the men inside the main building.

"Addie, how are you feeling?" I asked her as they laid her gingerly on a moth-eaten sofa.

Addie's breath was very sour. "These men say they've got the plague in the camp. They say . . . they say . . . it'll kill you. The plague . . . the plague is out of control. Is that true, Clint?"

I patted her damp forehead. "No, it's not out of control."

Addie raised her throbbing head, then rasped, "You're lying. The plague . . . the plague . . . is killing people. I don't want to die. I don't want it to kill me."

Over my shoulder, I heard Elsa's voice. "There's nothing like a panicky bird to upset things. I told you she was just a country bumpkin, a dull country lass."

I turned to face Elsa, my voice hard. "She's no such thing. She just needs some rest. She's had too much to drink. When she awakens, she'll be all right. Wait and see."

"I don't think so," Elsa said. "She'll get you in trouble, and herself as well. I find her cheeky, very cheeky, indeed."

The group of us, the reporter, the Dinka gentlemen, and I, stood around Addie as she lay there, snoring, with the rank vomit all over her chest. I closed her blouse and fastened a few buttons so her breasts would not flow out. Elsa got a big kick out of that and winked at me.

23

STEP LIGHTLY

A religious delegation, a collection of church officials from all faiths, came down to the camp, accompanied by two human rights representatives. The doctors suggested a meeting with them to air some of the pressing issues inside the camp. Reluctantly, I decided to talk with them. However, Addie kept out of sight, sending word to me that she was all right but didn't want to see me. That was fine with me.

The camp administrators ushered the church officials through the camp, pointing out its improvements and flaws, trying to put the bite on them for donations. Partnered with reporters and cameramen, the spokesmen for the various faiths set up shop in the main building, where the doctors resided and held meetings with officials.

After scrubbing up with a sponge and soap, I changed clothes. I'd lost weight with the food rationing and the restrictions on water. Sometimes I could hold my food down. Sometimes I was sick and had to hold my face in a pail kept just for that purpose. My belt was tight enough, inches less than my usual waistline, and I could feel my ribs poking through my flesh. Maybe it was parasites.

My meeting with the church officials was less than fruitful. Bishop Loso, originally from the border town of Nimule, did most of the talking. The rest of the elders watched my every move, hung on my every word, attempting to determine whether I had bad motives.

"We have a team of missionaries and representatives weighing the situation in South Sudan, assessing the need for supplies and funding," the bishop said. "I assured the camp administrators that we will help in any way we can. We're representing all of the parties involved here."

I nodded. "As far as I can see, these people are really in need of help. Not just more supplies, more food, more funds, but more staff. It's wonderful that the church is there for those in need."

"Praise be unto the Lord," Bishop Obote said.

Bishop Loso leaned forward and stared at me. "It's also the work to give comfort and hope to these poor, displaced people. These are our people. We have to make sure they don't give up hope."

"I understand that," I replied. "But sometimes when you have known so much suffering, your faith and commitment come into question. Most of these people have lost husbands and wives, children, homes, and now their identity. We must make them feel important and significant in the Kingdom of God."

"Very beautifully said," Bishop Obote said, glancing around at the other elders. The administrators, the doctors, and the media stood in the corners of the room, just out of earshot.

Bishop Loso, adjusting his tie, walked into the center of the space, smiling widely. "This is history, remarkable history," he said, striding proudly. "South Sudan is the world's youngest country. I've got roots in this region. It's celebrating its third birthday, and we have to expect some challenges in its infancy."

I rolled my eyes, thinking of the wretched people in the camp.

The arms of Bishop Loso went up theatrically as he recited some of the glorious moments in the fledgling country's past. "Reverend Winwood, you weren't here for the long, bitter struggle of this nation," he said. "There was no finer event than when the two opposing sides signed the peace deal in two thousand five, ending more than twenty years of civil war. Everybody in the south raised their hands to vote yes on the referendum splitting Sudan into two countries, one Christian and the other Islamic. The conflict is not only in the southern part of Sudan but in South Sudan. The violence has spilled over. The people started coming back from neighboring countries and this fighting and famine took root."

"And it's becoming very ugly," I said to no one in particular.

Bishop Obote, wiping a thin film of sweat from his collar, glared at the white men and their local staff across the room. "The government seems to think we can get along fairly well without the assistance of foreign aid organizations. Several attacks by the rebels have claimed the lives of European and American aid workers. However, some officials think the UN is a farce, sidestepping the crisis areas, where the need is the greatest. It always praises itself for its fine work."

"Do you feel that way?" I asked. "I disagree, because I see the staff of this agency risking their lives for people and countries without proper appreciation for their courage. I don't see them avoiding risk. They put their lives at risk every day."

"Maybe so, but these organizations are making a lot of money on our misery," Bishop Obote snapped, noticing one of the staff members physically restraining an agitated doctor.

Bishop Loso grinned deceptively. "Why are you here, Reverend Winwood? What purpose are you serving here?"

I glared at him, words failing me for an instant.

"Maybe I should ask, why are *you* here?" I retorted. "It seems that the regional church has failed these people, who are suffering mightily. The government doesn't care about them. Still, you seem pretty self-righteous about your role as a church in this country, as you call it."

Almost on cue, the bishops sat down and stood up like jack-in-the-boxes. They shouted at me as if I were a sinner, calling me blistering names in their native tongues and in English. They blasted me as a meddling outsider, a scoundrel for Satan, and an undercover agent for the murderers of Allah. Everybody hated Americans. They criticized me for being American as well.

Afterward, the church officials discussed with the doctors the need for more funding and supplies, and the medical team explained that two more isolation wards should be constructed to house the cholera patients. I noticed the church officials' affluence, their nice suits and shoes, the fact that they were traveling with security. One member of the medical team quietly pointed out to me that nearly half of the population lived in poverty, but because these guys had ties with President al-Bashir's National Congress Party, they lived much better.

"I would not doubt some of these church officials are spies, collecting information for the government," the medical team member said in a low voice. "Their positions are assured and protected. None of their churches have been touched."

I realized why the church officials had been hard on me. If outside aid organizations left and went home, the churches, established with the government, would have more clout and influence with the government.

"That's why the church officials resent you," explained the medical team member, a man from the Nuba Mountains who had joined the fight against the north. "You're a threat, as are all of us. They really would like us to surrender."

I was miffed. *Why are you here?* I wondered.

"Also, they play both sides. They are very friendly with the South Sudanese rebel leader Riek Michar and the South Sudanese president Salva Kiir," he said. "Last May the UN said both sides were doing war crimes and crimes against humanity. Your government has issued economic sanctions against both sides. That's why both sides do not like America and foreign criticism."

I nodded. "I see."

"There are a few foreigners in the camp, and I always tell them to be very careful," the medical team member warned me. "Like your friend, the woman, she should conduct herself better. She should know better."

"You mean Addie, right?" I asked him. I thought about Elsa's warning as well. Addie was getting in over her head. She didn't know the players or the political situation.

"Yes, the woman is playing with fire," he answered. "She's being foolish. She thinks everybody is her friend. Not so."

"What do you mean?"

"Reverend, she can get hurt or worse," he replied. "Watch out for her. You're her friend. Be her friend. Warn her."

"I have tried to warn her," I said sadly. "She's stubborn."

Before the medical team member turned to walk away, he reminded me of my duty as her friend and of the bad reception with the Sudanese church officials. He touched me on the shoulder and said, "Go and find her. Tell her not to play with fire. I would do that. I'd find her and give her a stern warning."

Later that day, in my tent, I dropped to my knees and prayed. I prayed for these refugees, with their hard lives filled with suffering, I prayed for the doctors and their staff, and I prayed for us, for Addie and myself. *God, protect us.*

While some in the church in Sudan worked hard for religious equality, there were those who had aligned themselves with the government. They knew their partnership would be fruitful, given the military might of the ruling government. It was like what had happened during the civil rights campaign in the United States: some of the churches, especially the black ones, had stayed out of the fight. The churches had chosen to let others do the hard work, but they had still enjoyed the benefits.

That evening, as I was walking back to my tent with my supper, I ran into Elsa, who gave me the latest on the cholera outbreak. She was considering a trip to Sierra Leone or Guinea, to check on the refugee camps there and the political mess.

"Have you seen your girl?" Elsa asked me.

"No." I was wondering if I should tell her about the warning I had got from the staffer.

"She was out with those guys again," Elsa reported. "She's seeing a lot of them. I don't think they mean her any good."

"I tried to tell her about her behavior," I said. "She's very stubborn. It goes in one ear and out the other. She tells me that she's grown and can do whatever she wants."

Elsa lit a cigarette and frowned. "That attitude out here can get you killed. She came out here with you. You need to tell her about the possible consequences of her actions."

"Again, I tried," I insisted.

"Also, she cannot hold her liquor, and the guys know it," Elsa added. "They get her drunk, and she acts like a tart. She's getting a reputation."

"I didn't know that," I said sadly.

"Do you want me to talk to her?" she asked.

"Elsa, do you think it'll do any good?"

She shrugged. "It might."

"Well, I guess it can't hurt," I concluded, worried about my friend, my formerly humble country friend. "Go easy on her, or she'll resent what you say."

As Elsa walked with me toward my tent, she said that she would welcome a change from Sudan. Along the way, we waved to the guards who were going out to patrol the perimeter of the camp. They were armed and carrying their food.

A second later Addie strutted past us, giving us a sour face. I told Elsa that I would see her before she left the camp, and then I approached my friend.

"Addie, can I talk to you?" I said, matching her step for step.

"What do you want?" she growled.

I grabbed her hand, and she yanked it away.

"What do you want, Clint?" she repeated as she picked up her pace.

I blocked her way, bringing her to a halt. "Addie, I'm worried about you," I said. "You're behaving quite recklessly. You're getting a bad rep around here, and you don't need that."

Addie bristled, leering at me. "Who said that?"

"It doesn't matter who said it. I just want to warn you that your actions can get you hurt here. I care about you. I worry about you."

"I bet the white witch told you that," she said. "I'm an adult, and I do what I want, talk to whomever I want, drink what I want. Go do your pastoring elsewhere."

I held her by the shoulder while others walked past us on their way to their duties. I wished I could make a dent in her stubbornness. I knew it could do her harm.

"What do you want, Addie?" I asked her tenderly.

Her eyes possessed great sadness and pain. "I want to go home. I hate this place. I wish I'd never come here."

"I'm trying to arrange that," I said. "It'll take a little time, but we'll get out of here. Be patient."

She stepped back, her eyes almost brimming with tears. "I don't know if I can do that. I'm restless. I can't stand still."

"You must. And you must behave yourself. Please, do that," I said. And then I walked off, carrying my supper.

24

WE CRIED HOLY

It was raining that weekend. It was a freakish down-pour, as it was not the region's rainy season. Dr. Bromberg approached me near the sheds about conducting a funeral service for some of the cholera victims. He told me that the burial site was a long distance from the camp and that they had to observe safety precautions during the service, in order to comply with the World Health Organization's regulations for the disposal of bodies. Still, he felt it was important to have a funeral service, to keep to the cultural traditions in caring for the dead.

"Would you do the honors at the funeral?" Dr. Bromberg asked me.

"Gladly. I'd be proud to do it," I replied.

The doctor then explained that private donors had provided the camp's stainless-steel postmortem tables, wheeled trolleys to transport the dead to the temporary mortuary, heavy black plastic sheeting for privacy, and body bags suitable for the outbreak.

"We're running out of room," Dr. Bromberg said. "Some families deny their relatives are dead from such a disease. Others hide them away. The families who acknowledge their loved one has been claimed by cholera want the body buried with a sense of dignity. You've made a lot of friends in this camp. Many people think you're a fair, honest man, unlike some of the church officials around here."

I smiled humbly. "Thanks."

"We want to give them a simple service, nothing elaborate, but reverent and respectful," the doctor said. "The camp administrators approved a ban of common graves and mass cremations, but time and space prohibit that action. Still, we want to do everything by the book. You're just the man to do the service justice."

His arrival probably timed to add some weight to his fellow doctor's sales pitch, Dr. Arriale joined us, pulling up a seat. He spoke to me like a friend from the old neighborhood.

"Can I say this?" he said. "I don't agree with the church officials' harsh treatment of you. What you don't understand is that some Sudanese officials hate any foreigner criticizing them. By the way, are you going to do the funeral?"

"Yes. I agreed to do it," I answered.

"Very good," they both replied in unison.

"Is my life in danger?" I asked them. "Will it be in danger during the service?"

"No, Reverend," Dr. Bromberg said.

"Addie, my friend, is freaking out about this cholera thing," I said. "She thinks she is going to die from it. She can't understand why more can't be done for the infected people."

Both doctors laughed, as if they had heard some smutty joke.

"All I can say is prevention is better than the cure," Dr. Bromberg observed. "If she is panicked about cholera, she needs to take every precaution. If she wants to ensure her health, she cannot be lax with her hygiene, and she should be careful with her associates. We'll do all we can do on our end."

However, Dr. Arriale added a somber note about the fear and stigma associated with cholera victims. "I feel badly for them. The victims of this horrible disease are shunned, rejected, by both family and friends. Sometimes even after they have been treated successfully at the hospital, the family isolates them, afraid to get the disease. Often we have to go into the villages and locate the sick, since their relatives hide them."

"It was like this some years ago, when we had the large AIDS outbreaks in Central Africa," Dr. Bromberg said. "The families don't want to touch or go near the victims. Also, they feel they will lose status and respect in the community if it becomes known that someone in the family has the disease. This is why we try to integrate patients cured of cholera back into the community, allowing the family members to see that they are cured and are able to resume daily life." He paused. "So, the answer is, you have nothing to worry about. And neither does your friend. If she would like, I'll give her a hygiene kit with water purification tablets and a special soap."

That gave me comfort. "I think she'd like that," I said.

"Any other questions?" Dr. Bromberg asked.

"It seems like a terrible death," I said. "One of your staff members told me it's very quick. Some people die within a day. How can you treat something that moves so fast through the body?"

"We do all we can to relieve the person's suffering," Dr. Bromberg said. "We do all the needed treatments and hope for the best. Sometimes the treatments fail, but more often they succeed. When they don't, we bathe the bodies in bleach, seal all the orifices, and put them into sealed body bags to contain any contamination. Cholera is no joke."

Dr. Arriale scooted closer to me, then spoke slowly. "The funeral will be a dignified affair. All family members and staff will be situated a distance from the burial site. You will be on a small knoll above the burial pit, which will be prepared and secured beforehand. We have to take measures not to corrupt the soil after the bodies are interred."

"We can't bury them near any water source, because the bodies could leak into the water that people bathe in, drink, or use when cooking food," Dr. Bromberg explained. "Those who are grieving will sing, hold lighted candles, and speak about their loved ones. Many of the people will stay away, but a large number will come as a way of showing that the community shares their grief."

"I like that," I said, nodding. "It shows that their loved ones are still a part of their lives, despite their passing. They live in our memory."

"Any more questions?" Dr. Bromberg asked. "I want to make sure that you know what you're getting yourself into. But I want you to know that everything will be done to ensure your safety."

"One last question. Can staffers be exposed through direct contact with a victim's body and soiled clothes and then contract cholera?"

"Yes, but we don't let that happen," the doctor replied.

With the matter of the funeral settled, I went back to my tent and prayed for several minutes for strength and courage. I didn't want to let the doctors down. The service should be something memorable and comforting to those whom the victims had left behind. But first, I had to prepare a sermon that gave hope to these poor souls. The theme of suffering had been on my mind full-time since it was all around me, in the camp and in the troubled land.

The sun was shining bright on the afternoon of the funeral, which was held the next Sunday. Four guards accompanied us—the doctors, a few members of the staff, and me—when we traveled by truck to a remote part of the wilderness. Workers had prepared the burial site for the victims, taking all the safety precautions. The family members and friends of the victims were treated with respect by all who had gathered, including other refugees, maybe a hundred, who came with candles and took their place a safe distance from the grave site.

"Reverend Clint Winwood, our American friend, will officiate at this funeral," Dr. Bromberg said, introducing me. "We're lucky to have him. A few of you already know him, since he has been visiting the camp. Give him a warm welcome."

A case of nerves assailed me every time I stood in front of a group of people, especially at weddings and funerals. I didn't know if these people would understand me. The doctors had assured me that many of them understood English, because of the American and English missionaries in the area. I was counting on that.

"My friends, my days in Sudan have shaped and strengthened my faith," I began slowly. "I've witnessed such courage and persistence among you, the families of the departed loved ones, the valiant doctors, and the medical staff. You all are so brave and fearless in this time of trial and suffering." I glanced at the solemn family members, who were clutching candles, their Bibles, and the memories of their beloved intact.

"We live in a time of great suffering," I said, adjusting my collar. "If you live this life in Sudan, you will face suffering every day. Everywhere you see suffering. Everywhere you see suffering taking a great toll on body, soul, spirit. There is nothing fair about suffering. There is sometimes no rhyme or reason with suffering. We try to control suffering, but it has a mind of its own. A good heart or good works cannot defeat suffering, as you know."

There was a smattering of sobbing out in the crowd. I turned to see the doctors and the staff fighting back tears.

"But faith can soothe suffering," I said, pointing to the mourners. "The Lord tells us He will ease our burdens if we only believe in Him. For every person, especially those who believe in Jesus Christ, He says you will have your share of trouble in this world. Believe in Him. He is the God of love and mercy."

I saw some of the children tugging on the legs of their parents and the old bracing themselves against the young. This was life in its real state.

"There are those who want to say our God is responsible for our pain and suffering," I continued in a stern voice. "There are those who want to say God is punishing us. They say we are following a false God. They say we believe in a God who is harsh and stern, who wants us to suffer so we can believe. These are all lies by the nonbelievers. They are evil and have brought hate and malice into our world. But God will not permit an evil, sinful world to rule endlessly. Their time will come. Remember that!"

At that moment I noticed that the doctors were getting impatient. They needed to get back to work, and the heat was a killer.

"Find comfort in God's plan of salvation," I said, starting my wrap-up. "As the good book says, in Philippians one, twenty-nine, 'For unto you, it is given in behalf of Christ, not only to believe in Him, but also to suffer for His sake.'"

As I was starting to get really revved up, I noticed the doctors' hand signals. They were urging me to finish my sermon. I'd forgotten how much I loved preaching. When I got home, I had to get back to the pulpit.

"Remember that God is in control of all life and that we are God's children," I said, concluding the sermon. "He is merciful and caring. His ears are open to our prayers. We are dealing with Satan and evil men who want to crush our souls. With God's help and guidance, good can result from suffering. Remember that. Don't be discouraged about the future. Life will get better. It always does. God is a living God. Pray for peace, pray that justice will be done, and pray that righteousness will stand strong and triumph."

When I finished my sermon, they clapped and shouted. I left the stage, totally dumbfounded, and made my way back to the truck. Dr. Bromberg said the final words, comforting the families of the victims and offering hope that those who had been displaced would return home soon. Sweat seeping through my shirt and pants, I sat in the truck, fanning myself with an old copy of *Elle* magazine.

25

RECKLESS

This was the day on which I wanted to have a showdown with Addie. My recent talk with her had had no effect on her reckless behavior, she had become the joke of the camp. I had thought that maybe Elsa should talk to her as well, but I now ruled out that idea. If things went really badly, then I'd bring in Elsa for a woman-to-woman talk as a last resort.

Since the day before the funeral, I had not seen the country gal anywhere. I ran into her Dinka friend as he was oiling his weapon near the shed that housed the generators, and spoke to him. Elsa was right. He was a mountain of a man, big arms and legs, a Paul Bunyan type. His appearance conflicted with his temperament, because he was a mild-mannered soul with a deep bass laugh.

"Hello. I don't know if you know me," I said. "I'm the reverend and a friend of Addie. I think you know Addie."

He laughed that booming laugh of his. "Sure, I know Addie. I know you too. You've been working with the doctors. People around here like you."

"Thanks for that," I said. "I've not seen Addie. Have you seen her?"

His face became serious. "Addie is a fresh girl. She's taken up with another guard, a bad man who likes to drink and mess around. She got tired of me. She wants fun and lots of it."

"What do you mean?"

"All the boys know her," the guard said. "If you're her friend, you need to tell her to stop the easy ways. They don't care about her. If they treat their women bad, just think of how they'll treat her."

A chill crept up my back. I was really concerned. I thanked him for his wise words, and then I set out to find her. This had to stop.

I didn't find her until late that night. It was after midnight. She was sitting on her bunk in her tent, dressed in her bra, which was stained with sweat and dust.

"Hello, Reverend. What can I do for you?" she said, giving me her sweetest smile. "I just got in. Had a great time."

"That's good," I replied.

Her brow furrowed slightly. She made no attempt to pull her blouse over her bare flesh. She seemed proud that she could tempt me.

"Everybody thinks I should warn you, Addie," I said. "You're running around with some bad men. These guys mean you no good. I told you that before."

There was nobody else in the tent. Everybody was watching the staff and the drivers play a midnight soccer match.

She put her hands on her hips and struck a seductive pose. "I'm glad I came over here," she said, winking. "I was a coward at home, and now I'm a lioness here. At first, I was nervous around men. I felt awful, but now I rather like it."

"Addie, you've got to stop this foolishness," I said strongly.

"Or what, Clint?" She glared at me with malice.

"Or something might happen to you," I said. "Sudan is not kind to women."

"Reverend, you know what I told you about needing attention," she said. "I love this place for that reason. I came down to the truck sheds, and the men went crazy. I never got that in Alabama. It's entirely sexual. They stared at me, wolf whistled, made bedroom remarks. I lapped it up. I loved it. It completely made me feel good about myself."

"The camp folks say you're violating their security precautions by traveling in the area at all times of the night," I said. "They don't want you to be a victim."

She looked in the direction of the camp's far entrance. "Don't pretend you know me. You don't have any idea what makes me tick."

"Most men have no idea what makes women tick," I answered.

"Clint, you're boring. You're afraid of women, love, and contentment. I told you this before too. I don't want a wimp. I want a hot-blooded man who knows what's what."

"What happened to you and the Dinka guard?"

"His name is Mickey," she said. "Like most Dinka men, he became jealous and mean. He wanted to own me. I told him I'm not his wife." Then she began to cry.

I stepped up to her and put my arms around her. "Addie, what happened to the good, old-fashioned country gal I knew in New York?"

"Clint, maybe something's wrong with my head."

"I don't know. I don't think so."

The tears flowed down her cheeks. "To be honest, I'm so confused. I don't feel right. I thought my life would be changed when I left the South. I couldn't wait to get away from there, but nothing changed."

"Sweetie, what's wrong with you?" I asked. "It seems like you're fighting yourself over something you did in the past. Is that it?"

Her arms went slack by her sides as her crying increased.

"I try to forget the past," she mumbled softly. "My father walked around the house in his drawers. You could see his thing. My mother was no better, walking around with her titties hanging out. My two male cousins stripped down to their drawers when they were in the house. I remember I was ordered to bring a bar of soap to my father in the shower. He would tell me that I wasn't seeing anything that I wouldn't see when I went out in the world. My cousin asked me to bring him toilet paper when he was using the bathroom. I saw everything."

"How did those experiences make you feel, Addie?"

"I got sexualized at an early age," she said. "I don't think I was ever a child. I developed early, getting curves way before my friends in school. My folks didn't talk anything about sex, but I was aware of it."

"Were your folks strict?"

"Oh yes, they were. They didn't let me go anywhere. While the other girls were allowed to date, my father kept me home. He kept me under lock and key. I was pleasuring myself like crazy. When I came of age, I left home with the first man who paid attention to me."

"Your husband, the one who died?"

"Yes, Clint."

She didn't stop crying. "Being with these guys and drinking doesn't make my inner feelings of being alone go away. I feel shame and guilt when I do this mess. But being bad can feel so good."

"You sound like you enjoy it," I said.

"When I get with one of these guys, I get a rush from the spark between us," she said, smiling. "It's almost like a high, a rush. I do it in the moment because it feels great. Sometimes I tell myself that I don't care what they think of me, but I do. Still, my body knows the difference, because my heart has no part in the sex."

I swallowed hard. "You've made a choice to have fun."

"I feel like crap after I do all these things, right after I'm with them, and I tell myself that I'm never going back," she said, wiping her eyes. "But the desire comes back full force later. Then I go and find the big black men."

"We've made a mess of us, huh?" I asked.

She sucked her teeth and spat, "Clint, you're a liar. You're a hypocrite. You don't mean the things you say. When we were in New York, you were all lovey-dovey, but here you act like you don't know me. I feel left out."

"But you disappear and nobody knows where you are," I replied. "You're good at vanishing. Somebody should know where you are all the time. This is Sudan, a very dangerous place."

Shrugging, she moved away from me, turned her back, and unfastened her bra. She knew what she was doing. She realized I was not going to take her to bed. She turned back around. Facing me, she stood there between the rows of cots with her full mocha-brown breasts exposed.

"I'm tired, very tired, sugah," she said, yawning. "I've got to get some sleep now."

26

WITHOUT CONSENT

That night was a tough one, for I tossed and turned into the wee hours of the night. I couldn't sleep. The elders talked about sensing that something wicked was about to happen and having that creepy feeling go through your soul. I sat up, wringing my hands nervously, as the sun peeked out above the trees. Eventually, I splashed water on my face, scrubbed my pits, and pulled on my shirt and shorts.

Spotting Dr. Bromberg on his way to breakfast, I caught up to him and walked with him. As we went, I discussed the crisis with Addie and our need to return to the States. He listened patiently, then said that a plane out of Juba was leaving in ten days. Maybe he could get us on that transport, with a little favor from the authorities. If not, Elsa says she can possibly work something with the officials she knows. Other journalists took the Juba route so they didn't have to deal with hassles from the government in Khartoum.

After breakfast, a meager meal of cornmeal and beans, I went with the doctor on his rounds. We carried our cups of hot, stout black coffee with us. After we stepped into one of the medical tents, Dr. Bromberg handed his defective stethoscope to a staffer, then put on surgical gloves and a mask.

"How are you, little grandmother?" he asked an older woman with matted hair who was barely alive on a stretcher. Her chest was trembling as she caught ragged breaths.

She whispered something to him that was barely audible. He patted her hand gently, trying to give her comfort. Then a staffer gave her an injection to ease her anguish.

I stood off to the side while Dr. Bromberg put another pillow under the perspiring head of a girl whose arms had been blown off by a land mine along the road. The doctor ordered two staffers to carry her to surgery. They would prepare her, lay in the supplies and meds, and the doctor would come later.

"Over the weekend we had several people injured by land mines that had been placed by the roads and trails," Dr. Bromberg said, standing near one of his assistants and checking a patient with severe stomach pain.

"Someone from security told me that they had swept the area for mines, but I guess they missed a few," I said, adjusting my mask.

"Indeed, Reverend," the doctor said. "I don't know if I told you this before, but the sermon at the funeral service was very fine. Good work."

"Thanks. Glad to be of service."

Dr. Bromberg pointed at another staffer and suggested he give a child a neurological exam, because the parents had said he was dull and sluggish. They had also noted that the boy couldn't keep food down or water. He had passed out three times in two days, causing some worry.

"Who are these girls?" the doctor asked, pointing at two young girls lying on a cot.

"Two Nubian girls from the mountains who crossed over from one of the border towns," one staffer noted. "A grenade exploded near them, and both of them are complaining of ringing in their ears. The taller one said she feels spacey—that's my word, not hers—and has a constant headache. We checked their ears and found slight trauma."

"What about the headache?" the doctor asked.

"We're looking into that right now," the staffer answered.

"And in the corner . . . What's going on there?" the doctor asked.

A woman was sprawled on a cot in the corner, her face toward the exit, one of her legs heavily bandaged. The wrapping was soaked with blood. Grunts came from her quivering mouth, between clenched teeth.

"A very deep machete wound on her leg," the staffer explained. "The wound is extensive, quite deep, through the muscle to the bone underneath. She was protecting her mother when the militia assaulted her."

"She's in great pain," Dr. Bromberg said. "Did you give her something?"

"In just a minute I will. I've sent for an injection of morphine," the staffer replied.

"That should give her relief until we patch her up."

Overcome by the whole drama going on around me, I stopped, took a deep breath, and let it out. These folks did this every day, day after day. I didn't know how they could summon the strength.

"Doctor, can I speak to you for a moment?" another staffer asked.

"Yes." The doctor stared up at the lanky assistant, who whispered that he couldn't stop the bleeding from a gunshot wound. The wounded young man, who had resisted the militia, had been shot twice in the stomach. The doctor went over to where the young man lay, pressed down on the injury, then asked for a sterilized needle and thread.

A row over, there was a teenage boy with pneumonia who was being given oxygen. The assistant administering the oxygen whined that the camp was running out of antibiotics. The doctor ignored him and continued mending the young man's wound.

Suddenly, two assistants ran over to a little girl in a tattered dress who had collapsed on the floor. Someone screamed, "She's not breathing!"

The doctor trotted over there, followed by me. The girl's skin was chalky, her lips were blue, and her eyes stared lifelessly up at the ceiling. A staffer began to work on her chest, doing CPR, pressing on her ribs, trying to force air back into her lungs. Another staffer injected her with something, and her pulse returned, though it was very faint. Finally, she gulped air, and they transported her to a machine to help her lungs function.

"Who is that kid there?" I asked the doctor.

"One family brought in this child with Down syndrome and wanted to leave him," the doctor explained. "They said the child was cursed with some voodoo, had a curse of some sort, and the family no longer wanted to keep him. They said the tribe shunned them because of the child. They left him in the care of the camp and wandered off toward the border."

The child, with the customary mongoloid face of those afflicted with Down syndrome, rocked back and forth near the doorway. He was agitated by the heat and the activity of the medical staffers as they went from one cot to another.

"You guys are good souls to do this," I said, pulling up a chair.

"All in a day's work," the doctor said, smiling.

There was a ruckus at the rear of the tent. One of the Dinka guards ran up to the doctor, waving his hands frantically, jabbering in his native tongue. The doctor listened attentively. A few of his assistants gathered around the guard, questioning him.

"Reverend, you should hear this," the doctor said, turning to me. "Your friend Addie has been abducted by one of the militias. There was an ambush. Some of our people were killed and injured. They took her, along with a guard and a woman from one of the border towns. We're doing all we can to get them back."

27

BITS AND PIECES

Immediately, the camp administrators and the doctors held a conference, which I was invited to attend, to see what they could do to free Addie and the others. The camp administrators insisted that they would not pay a ransom to any terrorists to secure the release of the three prisoners. The doctors contacted several faith-based organizations to explore all options, even contacts with the enemy side. Maybe they could find someone who could negotiate her freedom.

I was elected to call Addie's folks stateside to tell them about her plight. Only one of her aunts expressed concern. She worried that somebody would cut Addie's head off or hurt her in some other way.

"I hope they do something on her behalf, especially since she was working so hard to help those African people," her aunt said the second time I talked to her in two days. "Addie is a person who gives it her all. I know they appreciate all she did for them."

Little did she know that Addie had been unraveling before she was snatched. Drinking, carousing, and simply acting a fool. I didn't tell her this. I let her believe a lie.

"We have the American government and the UN trying to do everything to bring her back home," I said. "They know what these people want. They know how to deal with these people."

"I called the State Department after we first spoke, and the man say they don't pay money for any hostages," her aunt said in her Southern drawl. "That's what he said."

I couldn't let her believe that nobody in the government would do anything. The last time an American hostage was held, there was talk about private donors pitching in monetarily to secure the hostage's release or some trade of prisoners from Guantánamo. This was a mess. I had warned Addie about this foolishness.

"Reverend, I hold you responsible for her," her aunt said angrily. "She wouldn't have gone over there if it was not for you. She thought that if she went there, you would protect her."

"I'll do my best to get her back," I replied.

"That's not enough," she countered. "I want you to promise me. I want you to promise me that you'll get her back. Promise."

I didn't want that obligation. "I can't promise."

"What did you say, Reverend?" she said, barely containing her temper. "Why can't you promise?"

"Because this place is hell, and nobody knows what these demons will do," I explained. "You've read the papers. They're killing whole villages, killing women and children. I don't know what they will do."

I heard the sound of a newspaper being crumpled. Addie's aunt cleared her throat, trying to compose herself. "The newspaper said a suicide bomber went into a mosque and started shooting worshippers," she said. "They killed more than seventy people and injured about thirty. Then the killers set off bombs that murdered the people sent to help the injured. Is that these people who got Addie?"

"No. Those killers are in Iraq," I replied.

"Who are these people who got her?" her aunt asked.

I explained that these kidnappers were Africans, worshippers of Allah, who were trying to get rid of all

Christians. They had been at war with the followers of the Lord for years. That seemed to satisfy her for the moment. She was pleased that Addie was a warrior of Jesus Christ.

After the call, the doctors escorted me into the main building for a meeting. Elsa was going to speak about her contacts on the other side. We made our way to the back of the building, to a room that resembled a classroom, and sat down at an oval table. A large map, on which various routes to the rebel-held territory were highlighted, hung on the far wall. On the blackboard at the front of the room was scribbled the locations of the last known enemy activity. This information had been furnished by the authorities, for whom this whole affair was an embarrassment. They thought that it was best to avoid any trespass against Americans, unless someone was trying to make a point. "Let sleeping dogs lie," was their motto.

"I wonder how much money they would take for her," Dr. Bromberg said to Elsa, who had some experience in this area.

Elsa lit a cigarette and let the smoke drift out of her nostrils. She walked around to the blackboard and examined the list of sites where the enemy was holed up. Her eyes took in every detail on the map as well.

"You know, only America and Britain do not pay a ransom for their hostages," she said, scribbling down notes. "Now, if Addie were European, a deal could be made. Some European nations are not too proud to bail out their citizens. I know Italy, Spain, Germany, and France have done some back-channel deals to get their people free."

I knew she could present a pessimistic view of things, but I realized she was right about this thing. And I would be willing, if I was asked, to deliver a couple of suitcases packed with cash to the killers in the bush or in the desert. Her aunt was right. I did feel responsible for Addie.

"However, I can imagine that if every country started paying off these nutters, then things would get a bit crazy," Elsa mused.

Dr. Bromberg was drinking a glass of something with alcohol in it. I couldn't figure out what it was. Dr. Arriale looked at the new armed recruits, eight soldiers sent from someplace along the White Nile, then grunted and filled his pipe. Possibly he was thinking, like I was, that the enemy would ask for a large sum of money and then would kill Addie, anyway.

"Not that long ago, four French journalists were freed after being captured in Syria," Elsa said. "France said they did not pay anything for their release, but most people in the media know they paid something. It probably cost them a pretty penny."

"So it can be done, the freeing of an American hostage," I said, hoping against hope. "But how can we do it?"

Dr. Bromberg sipped his drink and frowned. The tension and anxiety in the room were rising. Nobody could say how a positive outcome could be achieved in this depressing situation.

"First, we have to find intermediaries, go-betweens, to act on our behalf," Elsa said. "Second, we must find someone who is trustworthy and is able to act with a sense of loyalty to our cause."

"Or Addie is dead," I blurted out.

"I hope these people are reasonable," Dr. Bromberg said. "With Isis, being an American or a Briton means death. I think we have to find out what faction took Addie and the others. Once we know what they plan to do with the hostages, then we can start to negotiate."

I was itching for a cigarette. "Is that right, Elsa?"

"Yes, for the most part, but some of these militias are fanatics," she said. "They would kill Addie and the others just to make a sick point. And then they would use the money to recruit, buy more arms, and stake out their territory."

"How is Addie's family holding up?" Dr. Arriale asked.

"The family is concerned and wants to get this thing over with," I said. "They're afraid for her safety. I don't know if the American media has been called in."

Elsa puffed on her cigarette, then stood next to the soldiers. "Have you notified the U.S. State Department?"

"Oh yes. I did that as soon as I learned the news," Dr. Bromberg said. "The officials said they would get back to me and that they handle such situations on a case by case basis. They asked me not to go to the press."

Elsa cracked up. "This is the story of a lifetime. It just fell in my lap. The press is involved. I won't call London until I get something solid."

"I appreciate that," I said, smiling.

"But then I've got it exclusively," Elsa said. "Agreed?"

All of us agreed. If Elsa could help us in our quest to free Addie and the others, then it would be worth it.

"But where do we find these go-betweens?" Dr. Bromberg asked.

"I know somebody," Elsa stated.

"Who?" We all asked at the same time.

"Bishop Obote," she answered. "He has all kinds of contacts. He knows the government officials and the rebels. He plays both sides."

"But he doesn't like me one bit," I said.

Dr. Bromberg dismissed that notion, saying it could have been male bravado. He added that he knew the bishop didn't like Americans, since they meddled in everything around the world. Also, he thought they were pious, self-righteous, arrogant, and concerned only with themselves. He especially hated George W. Bush.

"Do you think Obote would do it?" Dr. Arriale asked Elsa.

"He might, for a little bit of the take," Elsa replied. "It would have to be worth his while. He's a man who doesn't like to get his hands dirty."

"I'd like to talk to the survivors of the ambush," I said. "Can somebody arrange that for me?" The only bright spot in all this was that some of the soldiers on our side had interviewed one of the survivors of the ambush. He and the other survivor, both of whom were Addie's Dinka pals, had played dead after they were shot by the militia. They were recuperating at a clinic somewhere through the bush.

Elsa said she would check into it, and she volunteered to come with me. She warned me, however, that this excursion might not be easy to arrange but then noted that some people always wanted to score favors with the West.

"Now we're on track," Dr. Bromberg said. "At first, I thought this was a lost cause. I liked Addie and didn't want to write her off."

I was eager to contact some of the church officials from the south and ask them for assistance and guidance. They had been battling this war for some time. They had seen many of their number as dead or missing. They had seen their churches burned and their congregations scattered and slaughtered.

"We know there is enemy activity in this area," Elsa said. "We've seen the raids, the killings, and the burning of the villages. Sometimes they strike a series of villages and go across the border. They sell the women and girls. They turn the young boys into killers."

Dr. Bromberg set down his glass, grimaced. "I hope they don't harm Addie. I like her. She is a pleasant sort."

"I could take her or leave her," Elsa said and sniffed. "I don't think she's the brightest bulb in the marquee. A little too country for my taste."

Dr. Arriale smoked his pipe, filling the room with a peach-flavored scent. "You like the girl, right?" He asked, looking at me.

I ignored him at first, until Elsa coughed loudly.

"Yes, I do," I said, grinning.

"Is there anything serious between you two?" Dr. Bromberg asked me, refilling his glass.

I thought about that. "I like her, but I have been trying to figure her out."

"All women are mysteries, my dear man," Dr. Arriale said.

Elsa joked, "I think he figured her out and decided to return her to the shelf. She is a bit wild, even for him."

I shrugged. "Wild? I don't know." I didn't want to put all of Addie's business in the streets. Elsa was wrong to go down this road.

"Addie has had the men panting and begging to be with her," the reporter added. "I don't think she's the reverend's kind of girl."

I stood up, nodded to the doctors before leaving. "When all the arrangements are done, please notify me. I'll be working on my end. Thanks for the meeting. I'm extremely hopeful now."

28

WE SHOULD CARE

Word reached us that one of the militias had executed several villagers near a wall. They'd placed bags on the villagers' heads, and then they'd shot them. Three of the slain men had signs around their neck that said INFORMANT, because of their association with the government. I was panicked. I wanted to know whether Addie was a collaborator, according to the enemy.

Elsa notified me that a friend of hers in the security division of the government had arranged a meeting for us at the clinic where the survivors of Addie's ambush were recovering. Elsa denied that she was sleeping with him. She and I drove in a jeep with two armed guards through the bush to the clinic. I was afraid of what they might tell me there. I hoped Addie had not been harmed.

The clinic was ringed by guards and two armored trucks. We walked to the security checkpoint, presented our identification, and were allowed inside. The odor of decaying flesh was unbearable. I looked for the injured guards, the survivors of the ambush, but couldn't find them. One of the nurses pointed them out, and we went over to them.

One guard was worse for wear. He had taken three bullets in the chest and arm. He was in intensive care, due in part to all the blood he had lost, and was still unconscious. But the other guard was alert and talkative, although he had been shot in the shoulder and legs. He seemed glad to tell all he knew about the massacre and abductions.

"What were you doing there?" Elsa asked.

"Addie wanted to see some of Sudan's nightlife," the guard said, coughing. "She wanted fun. She wanted to see something other than the pain of the camp."

"Where was this place?" I asked.

"Just a place where men and women get together," he said, coughing again.

"Did you know the place was going to come under attack?" Elsa asked. "Who tipped them off?"

"I don't know, and that's the truth," the guard said.

"Had you been to this place before?" Elsa asked.

"No. This place just opened," the guard said. "They used to have a live band, but they stopped that because it was dangerous. The people danced to records on a dance floor. It had a bar with rooms where couples could get together upstairs."

I was curious about what had happened during the attack. And Elsa didn't want to get impressions; she wanted details. I knew the clinic's doctors were not going to let us talk to him for too long.

"How long had you been there before they attacked?" I asked.

The guard wiggled uncomfortably from the pain of his wounds. The staff at this clinic was not generous with painkillers. They did just enough to keep the patient from dying or from becoming a raving maniac.

"We had been there for about forty minutes before we heard the first gunshots," the guard rasped. "A man ran into the building, then dropped to his knees in the center of the floor. He couldn't get out the words to warn us. He was bloody. He had been shot many times in the back. Someone said, 'Cut the lights out, and hide in the corners, behind tables and chairs.' People trampled each other while trying to get out through the exits, and then they were cut down by gunfire. The women knew what was going to happen to them. They'd either be taken away, killed or, worse yet, raped."

"Were there any foreigners other than Addie at the place?" Elsa asked him. "I know a lot of aid workers like to let their hair down when they're not working."

The guard coughed deeply. "There were a few. Some of them were shot while trying to get to the bush. Those of us with weapons opened fire on the rebels, shooting bursts of automatic fire, but we were overwhelmed. They were too many of them in their Toyota Land Cruisers, and they poured into the building, shooting everything that moved. Some people they let go. I don't know why. But they searched for any foreigners after they secured the building."

"How did they find Addie?" I asked.

"One local woman told them about her," the guard said. "She pointed her out, saying she was American."

"How did they treat her?" I didn't want her hurt in any way.

"It wasn't just her." The guard's voice choked from emotion. "They treated everybody like animals. They looked in all the rooms, dragged everybody out onto the dance floor. They beat and clubbed them. One of the gunmen slapped this young woman until she bled from her ears. Some of the men resisted, and they beat them to the ground. We were marched with weapons at our back, two rows of us from the building. Addie complained to one of the gunmen about how they treated the women."

"That's Addie," I said, grinning. "Good old country spunk."

Elsa didn't see the humor in it. "Real stupid. Very stupid."

"The gunman got a wristlock on her and made her walk in front of him," the guard said. "She tried to yank her arm away from him, but he tightened his grip on her. You could see she was in pain. She didn't scream or cry out. She kept saying, 'You're hurting me. You're hurting me.' The gunman ignored her. The others with him laughed at Addie's whining. He shoved her against the wall, and they all started searching her body, lifting her dress. Her face was against the wall and her hands were behind her back while the men's hands moved under her dress. She tried to kick at them. They held her there while they felt her up."

"What else did they do?" Elsa asked. She was enjoying this part of the story.

"They got rough with her," the guard said. "When the men thrust their hands between her legs, she screamed for the first time. She tried to fight them, but they were bigger and stronger. She kept yelling, 'Cowards, cowards!' and 'Keep away from me!'"

"Did anybody try to help her?" I asked him.

"No. We wanted to live," the guard replied.

Elsa was practical. "That makes sense."

"The remaining foreigners and women were rounded up, bags were dropped over their heads, and their hands were tied," he added. "The rest of us they lined up against the wall of the building, and then they shot us. I lost my best friend. Elsa, you remember Cyrus. He was shot in the head right next to me. I lost my lady. They shot her in the neck and chest. They shot me many times. I lay there, pretending I was dead. If anybody moved, they shot them in the head. After they left with their hostages, I waited until morning and then I crawled off into the bush. That's where the soldiers found me."

"Poor bloke," Elsa said, stroking his head. His eyes were closed, and he was tearing up.

"I hate what happened," the guard said, fighting for his composure. "I have had nightmares about that night. I see my friend and my lady big as life. I can't get it out of my mind. It won't go. I will never get close to anybody else as long as I live. They ruined my life."

"Where do you think they took Addie?" I asked.

"I don't know," the guard said, his energy starting to wane.

"Has anybody from the camp contacted you?" Elsa asked.

"Dr. Bromberg called me this morning," he said. "They let me talk to him. He said they would give me anything I needed to get back on my feet. Also, the head of security called and told me to take as much time as I needed. They were kind to me. Everybody has been so kind."

"What will you do when you get out of this place?" Elsa asked. "Do you have any family?"

The guard stared at her sadly. "I don't know what I will do. I have no family. They have all been killed. Maybe Dr. Bromberg will let me stay at the camp. I won't be a bother."

A nurse walked up, carrying a pill and a cup of water. "All right, people. He's got to rest. If the questioning is over, then we'll let him sleep."

We said our good-byes. Elsa kissed him on the forehead and squeezed his bandaged hand. As the nurse walked us through the halls of the clinic, she expressed dismay about my kidnapped friend. She said she knew the situation would have a good outcome. What did that mean? I wondered.

Later, back at the camp, Elsa and I sat in the main building, comparing notes. We needed to decide how we would proceed. Nothing had been received from the rebels. No ransom note. No demands. Until we heard from them, we could not make a move.

"What did Addie's family say when they called?" she asked.

"They're talking with the government, especially the State Department," I answered. "Her aunt holds me responsible for this happening. She says I must get her back safe and sound."

"She's crazy," Elsa replied. "It's out of your hands."

"What do you mean?"

"If these people want to hurt Addie, there's nothing you can do about it," she said. "They're calling the shots, not you. Her family needs to understand that."

"I know that."

We sat there in silence in that suffocating space. A few minutes later Dr. Bromberg strutted toward us, wearing that goofy smile. Elsa frowned. We really didn't want to chat about our visit.

"How did it go?" the doctor quizzed us.

"He's hanging in there," I replied. "One guard is still unconscious and is in really bad shape. I think he's still in shock."

"Did he give you any information or leads you could use?"

Elsa lit a cigarette and faced the doctor. "He's lucky to be alive."

"I heard about the extent of his wounds," the doctor said. "He's a strong fellow. He'll pull through."

"Did you call the family of Cyrus?" she asked.

"Yes. All the arrangements have been made," the doctor said. "They have the body, and preparations are being made to bury him. We at the camp are going to help them in whatever way we can."

"That's good." Elsa liked that. She felt a fondness for the guards, who made it possible for the doctors and the staff to function.

"What about Addie, your friend?" the doctor asked me.
"He told me about the harsh treatment she endured,"
I said. "They took her, along with other foreigners, and
left. He said most of the people were lined up and shot.
Nobody knows where the gunmen have taken her. We
talked to soldiers, and they knew nothing."

The doctor put his hands in his pockets and rocked
back on his heels. "What are you going to do? Are you
going ahead with your plan?"

"I don't know," I replied. "I'm stunned by all this."

Elsa was adamant. "Time is of the essence. Either you
start putting something into action or the rebels will do
what they do. If you want to see Addie again, you must
have a plan of action. This is not a time to get lazy. You
must act now."

The doctor agreed. It was all on me to free her. "What
about the go-between?" he asked.

I told him that I hoped we could implement Elsa's plan
to have Bishop Obote act as the go-between to secure my
friend's release. We didn't know whether he would do it. I
knew of his dislike for Americans, but I believed he would
do this because we were both men of the cloth, warriors
for Christ.

"I'll contact him right away and get back to you," Elsa
said. "He'll probably ask you to meet him somewhere. If
you want, I'll go with you."

"Thanks for all your help," I said gratefully. "I couldn't
have done any of this without you."

29

THE FAITH THING

Working out an exchange for a hostage was tricky business. We still had not heard from the hostage takers, so we did not know what their demands were or if they wanted a ransom or anything. The American government said it was exploring various options for getting Addie out of the hands of the gunmen. Somehow Elsa's words rang true. Addie seemed to be on a reckless path. She seemed to be trying to find her way out of the Sudan madness, trying to have a little fun.

I couldn't accept that there was nothing that could be done for her. The State Department officials discouraged any attempt to raise a ransom for the kidnappers, because the cash would only encourage more abductions and fund more weapons for the rebels. What about Addie's family? What about her safety? I could not accept that Addie should die.

The words of her aunt kept returning to my head. "You are responsible for her being over there," she'd said, her fear rising. "She wouldn't be there if you had not gone. You must save her. You must do whatever is needed to save her."

Three days after our meeting with the doctors, I got a call from Elsa, who had flown to Khartoum to meet with Bishop Obote and other church officials. She said she didn't expect too much to come of their lunch. The

meeting had been secret, completely low key, because of
meddling by the security forces. She had been followed
from the time she arrived in the capital, and her telephone was being tapped. Still, Obote and the reporter
had eventually reached an agreement: Obote promised
to speak to me about getting my country friend released
and to act as my mouthpiece. Hopefully, Addie would be
freed.

I didn't see Elsa for a week after she got back from the
capital. And then we exchanged few words, as she had to
fly to Sierra Leone for leads for an Ebola outbreak story
that would air on the BBC. A call from her from Sierra
Leone ended too soon in a storm of static and silence.
She finally arrived back at the camp that Sunday without
fanfare and sent word that she wanted to meet with me.

"Reverend, we're going to have to keep this whole
affair a secret," Elsa said as we looked over the new
extension that was being built at the camp. "The bishop
wants everything to be very quiet. He agreed to act as the
go-between, but he wants a payment. I told him that you
are not a rich man."

"What did he say?" I asked her.

Elsa said he understood, but some formalities had to
be satisfied. "A fee must be paid in order for him to act
on your behalf. No rebel would respect him if he were not
paid for his services."

"I'll do what I can to raise the money," I replied.

Elsa stared into my face. "But then the rebels will ask
for another sum. I don't know what they will require. I
know they want to put you through your paces so they
know how much you value Addie. I ask you, is she worth
all you will go through?"

"What are you saying, Elsa?"

"How much do you love her?" she asked. "Is she worth
all the sacrifice, effort, and heartbreak you might go
through for her?"

"I know I must do something," I said. "Her aunt has gone public, telling *Good Morning America*'s Robin Roberts that Addie was an aid worker, toiling for the sick and the orphaned. She accused the U.S. government of threatening her if she tried to raise money for a ransom. Her aunt has retained a lawyer to handle any blowback from government officials."

Elsa slapped her forehead and laughed. "She is as much of an annoyance as Addie. She will get the girl killed."

"But that is not the least of the thing," I added sadly. "She is raising money to visit Sudan to meet with Western hostages who have been freed by the rebels. The meetings, she said, will put her at ease, as she will learn what is happening with Addie. The FBI has already contacted her about gathering information for them."

"I can tell you that the U.S. government will not attempt to rescue her," the reporter asserted. "Addie is not a big enough fish to warrant that."

"What else can you tell me?" I was eager to get any information she could give me.

Elsa was happy to relay the news of the capture of some rebel soldiers who took part in the abduction of Addie and the other foreigners in one of the South's tribal areas. According to one of the captured soldiers, the abduction of the foreigners was ordered by a head of the militia, who had been battling with the powerful forces of President Salva Kiir. The young soldier, who left the South Sudanese army for the rebels, suggested several hiding places where they could be holding the captives. There were many factions among the rebel force. Anyone of them could have her.

"Do you believe him?" I asked her.

"Who knows?" the reporter said. "These people switch sides at the drop of a hat. They want money, pleasure, and perks. The rebels promise them all the things they want."

"But what about the hiding places?" I needed to know there was hope. Maybe the South Sudanese government would respond and would rescue Addie and the others.

"An official from the army said they would check them out," Elsa said. "The army has its hands full fighting all these hot spots with various militias that are being armed by the government in the North. They are very unreliable. I wouldn't count on them to do too much."

"Who *can* we count on, Elsa?" There were too many players in the conflict in Sudan, with every region having its militia. The Khartoum government tried to control all of them with arms and money.

"Maybe Bishop Obote," she replied. "However, he has two masters, and we don't know which one he'll side with. The newspapers in Khartoum did an exposé on him and his lavish lifestyle. Most people don't know that he was in Egypt for much of his young life. His father was a supporter of President Nasser and later acted as an adviser to President Sadat, before he was killed. The bishop knows many of the players, as I told you."

"How can we trust him?" I wanted to believe in him.

"We can't," she said. "I laid out the entire story for him."

"The doctors said the bishop doesn't like me, so how do I know he will do the right thing?" I said. "It goes beyond the fact that I'm an American. Maybe it's because I'm a black American. Who knows?"

That perked Elsa up. "I think the black American thing is in your favor. The bishop is intrigued by you. He asked me a lot of questions about you and your life in the States. He wanted to know how political you were and what achievements you had in certain areas. Mainly, he wanted to know why you came over here in the first place."

I grimaced at that statement. "I told him that."

"He doesn't believe you," the reporter said. "He thinks you have some government contacts. He thinks you know some 'powerful and mighty people.' That's how he put it. When we were talking, I realized that maybe that's why Addie was snatched. He thinks you're a Yank big shot."

"That's madness," I retorted.

"Maybe that's why they're checking you out, Reverend."

"Checking me out? What?"

"When they decide on what's she worth, then they'll put together a ransom figure," Elsa said. "In these parts, money goes a long way. All these militias are competing for superiority and a chance to rule their little fiefdoms. In fact, I'm going now to cover the battle over an oil-rich area, Paloch. It's the last operating oil field."

I was alarmed since I didn't want to meet with the bishop alone. "When will you be back?"

"Reverend, I'll be back in three days," she said. "Then I'm going over to Somalia to see the fallout following the departure of Doctors Without Borders. They left in the summer of twenty thirteen, when it got too dangerous for them to operate. The agency had been there for over twenty years."

"What are you going to do there?" I asked, watching the refugees bake in the sun.

"I have some sources there, rebel and otherwise," she said. "I just want to look around to get the lay of the land. I haven't been there for almost a year and a half."

"What am I going to do?"

Elsa looked bewildered. "About what?"

"About meeting the bishop, Elsa. I don't know how to prepare for the meeting. What should I take? Should I get Addie's family involved? Should I get the U. S. government involved? What should I do?"

"No to your second and third question," she answered. "Go alone. Play it by ear. Flatter him. Make him feel like the big man. Stick to your guns. Believe me, the bishop does his homework. He'll know much more than he will say. Feel him out and set some rules."

"So no to Addie's family," I said, wondering what was right.

"No."

"And no to government involvement?"

"No. You don't want to get her killed," she said with a jab of her finger into my arm. "And these blokes will kill her. They'd kill her for sport, just because she's an American."

"It doesn't matter that she is black?" I said.

"She's not African, and what you black Americans don't realize is that being a Yank trumps you leaving in slave ships from the motherland hundreds of years ago," the reporter said sternly. "They consider you guys a willing partner in the American nightmare. You're like a distant relative who they really don't like or respect."

"Oh, man!" I exclaimed.

"I was in Syria when the rebels were attacking in the western province of Latakia and in towns north of Damascus, the capital. They were attacking the Christians who supported President Bashar al-Assad," Elsa said, lighting another cigarette. "Many times you Christians are on the wrong side. The Syrian president is a tyrant. He is a mass murderer."

"I know the man is a killer," I said. "But not all Christians support him. You're painting us with a broad stroke of the brush. Most Christians know right from wrong."

Elsa said she must have a talk with me and set me straight on the role of the Christian church in global politics. She accused me of being naive. She said this was because I was an American, and Americans had a self-centered view of the world. Her words left me feeling uneasy, for I really didn't know a lot about the planet I was living on.

"Did you say the bishop would give me a date for the meeting?" I asked. "Will he provide transportation?"

Elsa began laughing hysterically, coughing up smoke rings. "Reverend, I'd love to be a fly on the wall at your meeting with the bishop," she said, trying to catch her breath. "Don't make a fool of yourself."

30

DEAR ADDIE

The next few days were nerve-racking. There was a story in one of the local newspapers about a twenty-three-year-old Sudanese woman, Meriam Ibrahim, a Christian who chose not to follow the tenets of Islam and was sentenced by a lower court to death by hanging for committing apostasy, defection from Islam. This sentence was in keeping with the interim constitution of Sudan, which was drafted in 2005 and didn't allow for freedom of religion in Sudan. Meriam Ibrahim was given three days to renounce the Lord. In May 2014, while shackled in prison, she gave birth to a daughter. Only with international pressure was she freed the next month. She was rearrested the day after her release, freed again, and then she and her family took refuge in the United States embassy in Khartoum. After tense negotiations she and her family were allowed to travel to Italy and then on to the United States. The story in the local paper showcased what she was doing with her life in New Hampshire and her new liberty. It was a good read.

"Faith means life," Meriam had said upon her release from prison. "If you have faith, you are not alone." Faith was the main support that had sustained me in the aftermath of the loss of my wife and the children. I knew exactly what she meant.

A message came through one of the medical staffers at the camp that Bishop Obote wanted to see me the next day. The bishop said that there was no problem with the transportation, that he would provide me with a car and an armed escort. He was going to be at a camp near the White Nile, midway between several rebel strongholds and the bases for government troops. I prayed that night for everything to go well.

That next morning the car arrived with two armed guards to take me to the man who would possibly free Addie and the others. The drive was long and hard, the driver sometimes detouring around spots where there were mines and booby traps. A large part of the journey took us through the thick bush, and we motored into areas where ambushes and sniper attacks were highly possible. Eventually, we arrived at a camp, where the driver pulled alongside a large tent that was being guarded by a group of government soldiers.

I climbed out of the car and was quickly ushered into the tent. Inside it Bishop Obote sat on his throne, regally dressed in formal ministerial garb. He was a stout, dark man. His stubby fingers glittered with jewelry, and he had fashionable Italian shoes on his feet. His face resembled that of the noted late jazz trumpeter Clifford Brown, down to the pug nose and the proud mouth.

"I guess I asked you this before, Reverend Winwood, but why did you come to Sudan?" the bishop asked after he invited me to take a seat across from him.

"I came to Africa because I wanted to see the glory of the motherland," I replied. "In Harlem I saw a presentation on the troubles here in Sudan shortly before we left, the struggles between the Islamists and the Christians, the displaced refugees, the dead and the injured. First, it was the Congo, now this Sudan mess. My friend Addie first got the idea of coming here after going to a lecture on Sudan at Symphony Space in Manhattan. I came along to see that no harm came to her."

"Am I hearing you right?" he asked me. "You both came here as tourists, like on a sightseeing tour? Are you crazy?"

"No. That's not true."

The bishop leaned forward, his eyes blazing at me. "Then what is true? Please tell me."

"I was not an activist in the civil rights movement in the United States, nor was I a wild-eyed radical during the Black Power movement," I explained, looking at the bodyguard on the bishop's left. "I take pride in my past. Still, I plead ignorance. Most black Americans have little knowledge of Africa, and very few know any Africans, unless they're cornrowing their hair. In my youth I read with great interest about the emergence of the African nations and their push for independence. I loved the fact that Kenyatta, Nkrumah, Senghor, and others led their lands to freedom. I witnessed these facts with so much pride."

"But why did you come here?" the bishop asked angrily.

"I came here to see what I could do for Sudan," I answered. "I wanted to see for myself. I wanted to be a witness."

"What is your relationship with Addie, your friend?"

"Addie is my friend, and I am my sister's keeper," I replied.

"What is she to you?" the bishop asked. "Is she your lover?"

"No. I've not touched her."

"Is Addie a part of your ministry team, Reverend?"

"No. She's just a friend," I said. "I know her from New York, but you know all this. I've heard that you know all my history."

"Who told you this?" He pretended to be shocked.

"I can't tell you that," I countered.

Bishop Obote summoned a staff member to bring him a cool drink. He offered me one, but I declined. I could feel his eyes take my measure.

"What is your relationship with God?" he asked me.

I waited to reply until the staff member, who had returned with the bishop's drink, left the tent. I watched the bishop take several sips. He must have been roasting under those robes, but they made him look very imperial. He had to be sweating like a pig.

"I believe the history of the Christian church is a proud one when the church has fought for freedom and justice," I said firmly. "I believe God came among us in the person of Jesus Christ. I believe He died for our sins. I don't believe that Christianity has failed."

"Do you believe in miracles, Reverend?" the bishop asked.

I grinned widely. "I believe in miracles. Miracles happen every day. I believe in the miracle of God's love for His children. Many miracles have happened in my life. I don't question them. Miracles happen when a big obstacle is overcome without me taking any action. That's God's will. That's a real blessing from God, who loves us."

"What do you think is going on here?" he asked. "Be honest."

"The battle in Sudan is very complex, very complicated," I replied. "Those who are the faithful must wake up to the rising hostilities in the battle between good and evil. Christians who are strong in their faith will be punished and will suffer. The armies of evil are becoming stronger every day."

Now it was his turn to smile. His was a cruel smile. "Would you die for your God?"

"Yes, without hesitation."

The bishop ordered a man to bring him a tray of sandwiches, a plate of pastries, and another icy drink.

"Reverend, I think you're being dishonest," he said with an edge to his voice. "You're an American, and all that matters to you is making God obey your demands. You would love to overrule God's choices. You don't want to leave total control to God. That's just an American trait."

"That's bull," I retorted. "My belief in God has nothing to do with being American."

"I don't think so, Reverend."

"Here, I'm seeking your help to free my friend," I said. "You're telling me what I must do. I don't know what I should do. If I'm faced with a no-win situation, I'll pray and wait until the Lord speaks to me. When He speaks, I'll act on this crisis, and I'll know I'm doing the right thing."

Again, the bishop grinned cruelly. "How do you know it is He who speaks?"

"I know Christ speaks to me. That I know," I replied, fed up with him trying to get my goat. He really wanted to get under my skin.

The bishop snapped his fingers and whispered into the ear of one of his bodyguards. I couldn't hear his words.

"Reverend, do you know your Bible?" he asked.

"I do." What game was he about to play now?

"This is from Hebrews eleven, six," the bishop announced with a wry voice. "But without faith it is impossible to please him: for he that cometh to God must believe that he is, and that he is a rewarder of them that diligently seek him."

I sat there, waiting for the punch line. When the bishop remained silent, I said, "What are you saying, Bishop Obote?"

"Can you wait, Reverend?" He motioned again to the bodyguard.

"Yes, I can."

"Waiting means more than being patient. Waiting means that your time means nothing and that you are on God's clock. You can't make things happen according to your own timetable, Reverend."

I was so tired of his mind games. But I knew Addie's life depended on how well I indulged his whims. I had to endure this fool.

The bishop was handed a newspaper. It was in Arabic. He read aloud a story, translating it into English for me, about one of the local militias executing several of their men whom they suspected of collaborating with the South Sudanese government. A group of masked gunmen had yanked the supposed informants from a truck in the middle of a small town. They had ordered the alleged informants to lie facedown on the road and then had shot them one by one. The gunmen had later watched while a mob stomped and spit on the bodies and hacked them up with machetes. One of the so-called informants, supposedly the ringleader, was tied behind a car and dragged.

"Why are you telling me this, Bishop Obote?" I was alarmed, but I couldn't show it. I put on my poker face.

"I'm telling you so you know these people are not to be toyed with," the bishop said. "They are serious Islamists. They believe in their cause. Also, I read in the newspaper that Addie's aunt has gone public in the American media. She's stirring up a hornet's nest."

"I've not seen the papers or watched any television, so I don't know what she is saying," I said. "I cautioned her not to go to the media. I told her to leave the matter to the government."

"The government?" the bishop asked, snarling.

"Yes, I said that. I told her that I would do everything to get her niece home. I feel I'm responsible."

The bishop threw up his hands in disgust and then read something from a clipped article one of his bodyguards had just handed him. "Addie's aunt wrote this. 'I am sending you this message of hope and mercy. I don't know who is holding my beloved niece, Addie, but as her aunt, Gertrude Watkins, I pray that you show her mercy. I ask you to order that her life be saved. Addie did you no harm. She was doing humanitarian work in Sudan. She was helping the people in need. As her aunt, I ask your mercy. I ask that you not punish my niece for actions by our government or yours. She has always had a good heart and has always been willing to do for others. Doesn't the Prophet Muhammad say to reward good deeds? Doesn't Islam teach that no person should be held responsible for the sins of others? Isn't your God merciful? Please show mercy. We miss our Addie. Please let her come home.'"

I was furious. I had told her not to do this. I had told her that her big mouth could make matters worse.

"There is more," the bishop said in a mocking tone. "Aunt Gertie says she is very depressed. She told *CBS News Sunday Morning* that she sleeps in a darkened room, crying constantly. She can barely leave the bed and cannot eat. She said in the interview that she wants to die."

I kept shaking my head. *Such drama!* All she was doing was trying to get her niece killed for her moment in the limelight.

Satisfied that he had made his point, the bishop folded his hands and began his lecture. "The people who took Addie will test you. They will test your confidence, your faith, your courage. They will test you as a man and as a man of the Christian God. And every failed test will be taken again."

"I'm not some schoolboy," I blurted out.

"Didn't the great American minister Billy Graham once say, 'Closeness with God often means suffering with God for humanity'?" the bishop said. "I think he said that. If not, Reverend Graham should have said that."

"This is a joke to you," I said.

"No, it is not. We have one mission, and that is to get Addie and the others home. Alive. But, Reverend, do you think you have bitten off more than you can chew? Isn't that what Americans say?"

"No, I don't. I want to get Addie freed."

"We all do," the bishop said, grinning.

"Bishop Obote, can I ask you a question?" I asked. "Can I ask what faith you were raised in?"

"Good question. I spent my early years in Sudan, but my parents took me to Cairo, the Islamic world's largest city, and there I learned about life. My father was an aide to President Nasser and later an adviser to President Sadat, before he was killed. I became friends with the Islamists at Alexandria University and later at Cairo University. I followed the teachings of Prophet Muhammad strictly. However, something happened to my life, and I found Christ."

I was very curious. "What happened?"

The bishop was mum about that. "I don't discuss that."

"How did your father respond to your change of heart?"

"He didn't like it," the bishop said. "It caused a rift between us."

"It must have been difficult to go against your father," I said.

"Maybe I was never a Muslim," the bishop said. "Maybe I've always been a Christian in my heart. Some of my former friends consider me a traitor. Some say I should be put to death because I left Islam. However, I know it's my right to follow the religion of my choice. Everywhere you see this injustice. Look in Sudan and throughout the world. Leave Islam and die. I've put my life at risk for the Christians of Sudan. I know their suffering."

"How can you help me?" I asked him. "You're on the outs too."

The bishop took a sip of his beverage and smiled. "I can help. I still have friends here in high places. I still have friends among the rebels and the government. My name carries some influence."

"I hope so," I said nervously. "If not, Addie is dead."

"That won't happen," he said finally. He turned to one of his bodyguards and said, "Take him back to the camp." Then his gaze landed on me again. "Reverend, wait until you hear from me. Then you follow all my directions. If you do this, then we will get your friend back. Farewell. This has been a very interesting talk."

31

OUT FRONT

Elsa called me the day after my meeting with the bishop. She wanted to hear all about it, what I said, what he said. The Somalia trip had worked out well for her, with good interviews, informed sources, and fine interactions with government officials. What she informed me was that there was a high level of risk involved with me going into rebel territory to negotiate with the hostage takers. I could get killed.

"That's why I might have a surprise for you," she said.

"What surprise?" I asked. "I need some good news right about now. The talk with the bishop gave me chills."

Elsa told me I was not going to be alone when I went into the lion's den. A friend in the European intelligence community had informed her that they had an idea where Addie and the others had been hidden, but a raid in the small village would bring much bloodshed. South Sudanese soldiers had revealed that a group of foreigners had been sighted in a remote area controlled by rebel troops that were heavily armed and deeply entrenched.

"That is good news," I said, grateful for this report.

"Reverend, I got some assurances from the South Sudanese government," the reporter said. "It made an announcement that it will initiate 'a massive deployment of men and resources' to put an end to insurgent activities in remote areas of the country. I hope that means they will do something about the rebels."

I thought that might be trouble for Addie. "If they put too much pressure on the rebels, they'll kill the hostages. These thugs will kill them without fail."

"You're still worried about that country girl," she scolded me. "She didn't care about you. You're an honorable man. You deal with hearts and souls. Still, you ignore what she did to you. You refuse to look into her cheating heart."

My voice shook. "I know what she is, and I know what she was."

"What does that mean?" Elsa didn't like the country-woman.

I thought back to the good times in Alabama, when Addie had seemed to be a good-natured country gal. She had got me through some pretty tough moments. I had wanted to make her happy at first, had wanted us to be together, like we'd been back there in the boonies. But now she had gone rogue. She had gone man crazy. It was a matter of principle. Her actions had their fair consequences, but they had killed off any chances of a possible commitment.

"You know she asked for this mess," Elsa added.

"I know this," I replied. "Addie caused all this foolishness."

When Bishop Obote had asked me whether Addie was my lover, I hadn't lied to him. I didn't want to commit to her. Still, back in New York, we used to be able to discuss almost anything. However, she'd changed. As the old bluesman Jimmy Reed sang, "Bright lights, big city gone to my baby's head." I wished we could have talked about the more serious matters of life, experienced the joy of sharing feelings, ideas, goals. Lately, she had been a stubborn hussy, a tart, and our dream of real companionship had slipped away. I didn't want her like she was acting wantonly in Sudan.

"You know, the government wants to revoke my press pass," she said quietly. "They want me to plant a few positive stories and make them look good."

"Are you going to do what they ask?"

"No," she answered. "But you have more to worry about. You're right about these hostage takers. They are unpredictable. They can't be trusted. Also, the government in the North says Addie and you traveled without their permission. The officials say they didn't issue permits for you, as foreigners, to travel outside Khartoum."

"They're trying to cover their butts," I said.

Elsa laughed. "The government is trying to position itself in case the hostage situation goes badly. It says it doesn't care what America says. Still, it wants to keep itself on America's good side."

"Do you trust Bishop Obote?"

"The bishop always wants to come out on top," she said. "He had a hand in the Arab Spring. He's got ties to every camp. In Egypt he knows a few of the coup leaders who were trained in U.S. military colleges, as well as several old-timers from the Mubarak camp. I wouldn't trust him, although he can talk smooth and slippery, like a car salesman."

"I don't trust him," he said.

"I hope Addie has nine lives, because she'll need all of them," she said. "She's running out of time. Her aunt is talking her niece into a grave. It doesn't take much courage to talk when you are safe and secure."

"So what are you saying? That I'm not in this alone?"

"Reverend, you might get help, but you are going to approach them alone," she admitted. "Nothing happens until you make contact. You must engage them before anything happens. I have got some assurances, but you must go in there by yourself."

I felt a chill go through me. "What happens if the reinforcements arrive late? What happens then?"

"Then you're up the creek without a paddle," she said. "Are you afraid?"

"Heck, yes, I'm afraid," I confessed. "I don't know how I got into this madness. I'll admit it. The bishop warned me about the bogeymen and how they can be brutal."

"They're butchers," Elsa asserted. "They're fighting among themselves. They try to outdo each other with their savagery. These blokes are fiends who whip, beat, behead, and slice and dice their victims. They don't care about the West saying they've committed war crimes, crimes against humanity, torture, murder, and such."

I frowned. "The bishop told me this. He told me that they cut the hands off of men who are thieves, flog men who smoke or drink, beat women if they show their face on the street or get caught being intimate with other men. These men are laws unto themselves."

"What if they torture you?" she asked. "Are you prepared to die for your faith? Are you prepared to become a martyr for Jesus Christ?"

"The bishop asked me that question," I replied boldly. "And I answered yes."

"Suppose they torture you and don't kill you right away?"

I picture myself tied up, with one of the rebels snipping off my toes or fingers, slicing off my ears, ripping off my fingernails. How much courage would I have for the Lord? How much pain and suffering could I stand for the Christ who died for us on the cross?

"Reverend, you must consider all of this before you walk in there," she insisted. "This will not be a picnic. It could get nasty and bloody."

"I've prayed that will not be the case," I said.

Elsa had a little fun. "I wonder if Addie would do what you're about to do for her. I wonder if she would throw up her hands and walk away. Or would she walk right into the lion's den?"

"I don't know," I admitted.

"The bishop told me that he'll convey the details of the plan to you in enough time," Elsa said. "Someone will come to the camp with the message from the rebels. He doesn't trust the phones. He has alerted the camp to permit any communication between the hostage takers and yourself. There will not be a problem."

"Have you heard anything from the State Department?"

"No, not recently," she said. "I think they're mad at Addie's aunt for going with her story to the mainstream media. She went to CNN, and that is seen all over the world."

"I wonder how long they will make me wait," I said. "The bishop said that patience is a virtue in these kinds of things. I'm a patient man. But I can't wait forever. Who knows what they will do to Addie?"

That incensed Elsa. "You need to be worried about yourself, Reverend. Addie will take care of herself. Her kind always lands on her feet. You've got much more to lose than she ever had."

With that final retort, the reporter hung up. I sat there looking at the phone, wondering if Addie would respond to this crisis like I was doing if I were in her shoes. Or would she go on her merry way? I would never know.

32

THE TROUBLE I'VE SEEN

Shortly after the phone call from Elsa, I found a secluded corner in the main building, a small room, and entered and closed the door. I knelt on the hard wood, clasped my hands, and prayed like I'd never done before. I didn't beg or plead. I talked to God like he was my parent, my elder, my constant companion. Inside my head, I pictured him as the Son of God, with thorns on his bleeding head, his torso severely injured by a savage beating, his hands and feet pierced by huge iron nails driven into the wooden cross. This was the holy image I talked to, the divine Redeemer.

I spoke the prayer aloud, not silently within, on the blackboard of my mind. I wanted to hear the words. I wanted to taste the urgency and the power of them.

"O Holy Father . . ." I began the prayer for the Lord's protection with a focused mind.

Just then the roar of trucks penetrated the walls of the building. My ears tuned out the noise, but the powerful motors served as background music for my talk with the Almighty God.

"Dear Lord, my life has been turned upside down," I continued. "I know you use us, the little people, to accomplish the impossible. Lord, guide my steps toward, and not away from, those who need me. I know I'm not too badly shattered for you to repair. I know you love me, despite my imperfections and defects. Please use me to your advantage. Make me your servant."

Footsteps sounded in the hallway outside the door. I waited for the people to move away before I continued.

"The Bible teaches us that the Lord takes us as we are, but He never leaves us that way," I said quietly. "I believe that. I believe that He never leaves us the way he found us. The Lord found me after much sinning and backsliding. I resisted Him, coming up with all kinds of excuses, lies, deceptions. The world wasn't finished with me yet. It had a grip on me, and its embrace was firm and seductive. Before I married, I was desperate, praying for salvation and redemption. I was drinking and smoking too much. I loved the ladies too much. Still, I kept talking to the Lord, who refused to answer me at first, denying any communication with Him until I got my mind right. I wondered if all sinners had to go through this barrier. I wanted the Lord to make His presence felt in my life, and I wanted a touch of His divine wisdom, for I was running around in circles."

My head turned sharply when someone tried the door and opened it. A woman, a stout European lass with long blond hair, saw me, said, "Excuse me," and promptly closed it. I tried to find the thread of thought for my prayer.

"Maybe the Spirit brought me to this place," I continued. "Maybe not. As long as I have been here in Sudan, the Spirit has been with me, often through extreme times. Lord knows I've never seen anything like the happenings over here. Never."

A whiff of human sickness came through the open window. I swallowed, pinched my nose, and went on with my prayer.

"I remember my life has purpose and my faith is strong," I said. "Inner peace comes from the knowledge

that the Lord loves us and is in total control. Some folks
say that worry is a burden that God never wants us to
bear. Yet I'm worried about this outcome. I understand
that the Lord can create a road when you see only challenges and obstacles. Your power can overcome any and
all difficulties. As my late aunt used to say, 'Everything we
do produces consequences. Every choice has its reward or
punishment. Even doing nothing can produce a result.'
As a Christian, I will not postpone the blessing of action.
I will not postpone life."

I paused then. In the silence of the room, I became
aware of the ticking of a clock, the minutes and seconds,
the ingredients of life.

"The elders always speak of how we molded the agony
and suffering of our bondage and transformed the faith
of our captors into something we used to guide us on our
journey to our salvation and triumph," I said proudly.
"I believe in the dignity of the undefeated. I believe in
the dignity of the poor and the displaced. I believe in the
dignity of their joy and resurrection. I believe in their
unbreakable faith, their strength, and endurance. I believe
the Lord hears us when our pleas are heartfelt and our
need is great."

I paused and took a breath. I noticed then that my arm
had fallen asleep from supporting me. A moment later
I went on. "In Revelation twenty-two, seventeen, the
scripture says, 'Let him who thirsts come. And whosoever
will, let him take the water of life freely.'"

Again, the door opened. It was one of the medical
staffers. He said there was a messenger at the gate with a
letter for me. I told him that I wanted to finish my prayer,
and then I'd go down to see him. The staffer nodded his
assent.

"Hell is to be cut off from the Lord and His presence,"
I said. "Heaven is to know Him. Someone once said,
'Courage is fear that has knelt and said its prayers.'"

The staffer waited and let me conclude my words to the Lord. I was thankful to him that he was so patient.

"Under these oppressive conditions in Sudan, many Christians have lost their faith and think they must surrender to insult, injustice, and hate. Christianity and Islam are great religions. Historically, they carry in their holy books a message of goodwill, compassion, justice, and brotherhood. People with their own agendas have corrupted their messages. The madness in this place is not between Christians and Muslims. I've seen followers of both faiths, and by and large, they are good, hardworking people who are trying to survive on the land. The madness is generated by bloodthirsty extremists who refuse to let people worship the God of their choosing."

I felt the staffer's presence in the doorway. That didn't matter to me.

"Although this situation is dangerous, I feel an inner peace and the power only God can give," I said in a louder voice. "To quote Adam Clayton Powell Jr., 'There is no easy way to re-create a world where people can live together.' This is the case in Sudan, where prejudice, intolerance, and greed rule. Only God's warriors can put an end to the suffering. This violence is evil and immoral. The faithful must pray to Almighty God to stop the bloodshed and ease the hate. Christians must rise up. They can't remain silent or submissive."

Now growing impatient, the staffer coughed harshly. I knew I had little time to finish up.

"Freedom, as Dr. Martin Luther King once said, is like life," I said, concluding my prayer. "'You cannot be given life in installments. You cannot be given breath but no body, nor a heart but no blood vessels. Freedom is one thing—you have it all, or you are not free.' I trust the Lord. I know He will see me safely through this ordeal. Praise be to God. Hear my prayer. Amen."

Smiling, the staffer helped me up, then led me down the stairs and out through a side entrance. He pointed to a shabby child surrounded by a group of armed guards, their weapons trained on the thin figure. I ran off in that direction.

33

ONE WAY OR ANOTHER

Once the guards saw me, they backed up and let me speak to the child, who handed me a tattered, sweat-stained note and whispered something in my ear. Then he turned on his heels, shot a glance at me, and ran off into the bush. I walked back toward the tents, reading the note, trying to figure out what it meant.

If you wish, you can come for the woman and the others. We sell women. They are nothing in our faith. We make no promises, but we will receive you. Instructions to follow.

As I walked through the grounds, Dr. Bromberg waved to me, beckoning me to come into the main building. I mounted the steps to the building, and when I reached his side, he put his hand on my shoulder. We walked inside the main room, and there I saw Dr. Arriale, who was flanked by a white man in a rumpled white suit, his hair graying, two men in UN regalia, and a couple of medical staffers. I wondered about the man in the suit, because its fabric seemed too heavy for this tropical climate. Everyone was sweating profusely.

"Our embassy doesn't want to do anything to complicate relations with the South Sudanese officials," said the man in the white suit as he adjusted his wraparound Ray-Ban sunglasses. "They tried to pressure us into sharing intelligence about the increased rebel activity along the White Nile. No dice—"

Dr. Bromberg interrupted his statement. "What are we going to do for the minister?"

"What indeed?" said the man with the graying hair. He looked at me. "By the way, are you Lutheran, Christian Scientist, Catholic, or Presbyterian?"

"I'm Baptist," I replied proudly. I knew that in some circles Baptist was the lower rung of the religious congregations. A stepchild, an outcast.

The man with the graying hair went over and took a seat at the table. He was followed by the UN representatives and the doctors. "Reverend, I've passed your request for assistance on to Washington. Expect a decision on it shortly. Some things take time."

"Will I be safe out there?" I asked as I sat down at the table. "Who are you?"

"I'm a representative of the State Department," he said, suddenly removing his sunglasses. "I think you'll be safe. Our friends at the UN will be our eyes and ears here. We'll partner with them, and they shall give us every resource necessary. I wouldn't worry."

I addressed Dr. Bromberg, reminding him that the bishop had said that the U. S. government would be sending some assistance. The bishop knew every trick.

"How much does this Addie mean to you?" the government man asked me. "I know this bishop. You're dealing with the devil himself."

Dr. Bromberg scratched his head and frowned at this statement. "Isn't this a bit odd? Reverend, you're being emotionally blackmailed to do something you find despicable. I believe you're a moral man."

"Elsa asked me if Addie would do this for me, go into harm's way," I replied. "I told her I really don't know what she would do."

The government man shrugged. "These guys want something from you. They're using the woman as bait.

They want either cold, hard cash or a public relations victory. Have you slept with her? These bad boys will use sex as a weapon against unsuspecting civilians."

I bristled. "That's none of your business."

Dr. Arriale answered for me. "Elsa said he hasn't slept with her. As a man of faith, he refused her advances. She's a pretty wayward woman."

"Don't say that about her," I countered. "She's my friend."

"He's going to contact you, right?" the government man asked.

I handed them the note I had just received from the child, and they passed it around. Maybe the guy from the State Department could make out what that blasted thing was really saying. It really didn't make sense. What did they want?

"You think you know the bishop," Dr. Bromberg said, handing back the note. "He's completely corrupt."

"See? The bad guys believe they've got to our pastor already," the government man said. "To them, he's ripe for the picking. A lonely guy. A widower who lost his wife and kids. They've checked him out."

It was certain that Dr. Bromberg really didn't like the bishop. In his opinion the bishop did what most in the hierarchy of established Christians, the bigwigs, did: pandered to both sides, while ignoring the real needs of the poor.

"The bishop doesn't make mistakes," Dr. Bromberg noted. "He's very calculating. He'll come out of this thing smelling like a rose."

The government man stared into my face, his tiny eagle eyes piercing my resolve. "Maybe they want to recruit you. It would be a major coup for them. I could see them forcing you to act as a mouthpiece to the American media. That would get some attention."

"No way," I said angrily.

But Dr. Bromberg got on the bandwagon, agreeing with the State Department rep about the possibility of my doing a Tokyo Rose for the Islamist rebels. I would rather die than do something like that.

"He has a point there," Dr. Bromberg said. "It would be great to have an English-speaking, fallen Christian preacher spewing Islamic extremist gibberish. Get in and get out."

The government man asked the doctors for a glass of water, then continued. "Reverend, you cannot behave badly. You must try to tell the truth as much as possible. Then, when you tell a lie, they'll believe you. Don't let us down. Always keep America in mind. Don't bring your country disgrace."

"I won't do that," I replied. "I'm always loyal. I'm an American citizen first and foremost."

One of the staffers passed a glass of water to the government man, who sipped it like it was red Kool-Aid. "The bishop wants you to do what he tells you," the government man said sternly. "If you don't, he'll be very upset. He might make your life hell. The bishop doesn't like to lose."

"Keep your wits about you, and you'll be all right," Dr. Arriale said. I was pleased they were worried about my safety.

"These fellas'll try to work on your mind," the government man said. "They'll tell you a bunch of lies. We'll protect you, no matter what. You can be assured of that. However, the situation might get dicey, but if it does, we'll bail you out."

"Is Addie so important to you?" Dr. Bromberg asked me. I didn't like him messing in my personal business.

"She's my friend, Doctor." I tried not to get mad.

"Do you plan on marrying her?" Dr. Bromberg asked.

"I don't know," I replied.

I remembered the note and what the kid had told me. He'd whispered that I should burn the note after reading it. It might fall into the wrong hands. The bishop knew I would give it to anybody who could help me. I would give the note to anybody who would free Addie, because I was desperate and felt my back against the wall.

"I'm sure the rebels will know you gave it to us," the government man said. "They know what you do and say. They know we're here. This camp has several people working on their side. We know all their names."

"You do?" Dr. Arriale asked.

"Yes, we do," the government man answered as he stood to his feet. He caught my eye. "Look happy. Don't be so glum. You'll get her out. She'll be safe. Trust us to back you up. Still, keep your guard up. You'll be in terrible danger until we arrive. Don't get careless. Don't get reckless." He walked over to the briefcase he'd left on a nearby chair and pulled out a folder.

"I won't be careless," I said solidly. "I won't embarrass you guys."

"Are you worried?" Dr. Arriale asked me.

"No, not really," I answered.

"What if something goes wrong?" Dr. Bromberg asked.

"I'll deal with it," I said. "I have my faith to protect me. The Lord will shield me."

The government man walked back over to the table and spread something out on its surface.

"Gentlemen, these are some satellite images taken of where we think Addie and the others are being held," he said, holding one up. "The buildings circled with a Magic Marker are the prime targets. They're protected by the rebels, but our concern is for the captives. We don't want anything to happen to them."

I was astonished by the information he had revealed
to us. Usually, the government held its cards close to the
vest.

"We needed more men like you, Reverend, during the
Cold War," the government man said, laughing. "We'd
have beaten the commies easily."

"You said you had something to tell us about the security of the camp, yes?" Dr. Arriale asked the government
man.

"Oh yes. We have word from some sources that the
camp can expect to come under attack," he said. "We'll
send over some reinforcements to bolster your defenses.
Meanwhile, Reverend, you continue your routine as usual
until you get final instructions. When you do, notify us
first, and then follow the instructions of the bishop to the
letter. Again, we'll monitor your every move."

I nodded, taking every bit of advice.

Walking over to me to shake my hand, the government
man smiled with his eyes, as if trying to put a positive
spin on a bad situation. "Don't breathe a word of what we
discussed here," he said, pumping my hand. "Let's keep
it in the family."

34

AGITATION

Sometime in the middle of the next night, a strong hand shook me awake. I saw a shadowy figure hold a finger to his face, asking me to be silent and to listen. He stood just out of my line of sight after a time. But his voice, low and raspy, gave me a hint that my time had come. I was going to begin my journey to get Addie back.

"The bishop sent me, and now you will meet your lady friend," the darkness said, still asking me to be quiet. "There is a car waiting for you outside the gate. You will have no trouble from the guards."

I saw a ray of night light flicker across his face. It was one of the medical staffers, the assistant to Dr. Bromberg, and he was pointing the way to the car. No wonder the rebels knew their every move.

"Now, hurry," the staffer said. "Good luck!"

Scrambling to gather my things, I tucked everything in a small bag and ran to the gate. I reached the gate and nervously waited to be stopped, but the guards suddenly turned and looked the other way. As fast as my feet could carry me, I ran toward the car. The door opened, and I slid into the backseat.

"Quiet, Mr. Preacher. Not a sound," a child soldier said, placing an automatic pistol to my temple and handcuffs on my wrists. "Let's go. Get away from here quick."

The car's motor roared to life, and we sped away through the bush. Nothing was said. The rebels were well trained, obeying their orders to the letter. The handcuffs bit into my wrists. I had no idea where we were going. I lost track of distance in the total darkness, and the stretch of road ahead through the trees seemed endless. We changed cars after a few miles and drove for hours before another vehicle joined us. I could see its headlights dimly through the dust and blackness.

"Where are you taking me?" I asked the men.

Nobody said anything. The car kept on its path to its destination, where I hoped I'd find Addie and the others.

Suddenly, the cars pulled into a small village. Three rebel soldiers formed a roadblock, walked around the vehicles, and inspected them. When they saw me, they laughed and shouted in their language. The village was strangely quiet. It was as if its residents were trapped inside, prisoners in their homes, while the rebels patrolled the streets.

The vehicles rolled forward a few yards and stopped inside a large shed. A group of men escorted me from the car, with one smelly thug holding a weapon in my back. They took me to a room in a small building. My first instinct was to call for help, to scream bloody murder. But I realized it was futile for me to yell for someone to come to my aid.

"We got the big American preacher spy," one rebel yelled. "He fell for the trap, and here he is. Welcome to hell!"

For an instant, I thought about what the government man had said about the possibility of torture and whether I could withstand it. *Crack my skull. Pull out my fingernails. Snip off my fingers and toes one by one,* I thought defiantly.

"Why did you bring me here?" I asked them. "Where's Addie and the others?"

The men said nothing. I stood in the center of the room and waited for the head man to come. I could tell these folks were underlings, grunts. They talked among themselves before they searched me carefully. The one who spoke about "the American preacher spy" stepped forward and freed me from my cuffs. He spoke fairly good English. He asked me to undress. I protested, but a hard blow brought me to my knees. My head was spinning from the punch.

"I'll do it," I replied, my face starting to swell. "You don't have to get rough." I stripped down to my drawers, but they wanted me as naked as the day I was born. I complied with their demands.

After a time, they led me downstairs to a windowless cell, where I sat on a dirt floor. They hurled my clothes inside after me. There was a bowl for my toilet. No bed. No place to wash up. That first night I huddled against the wall, wondering what would happen next.

The next morning I said my prayers, and then they brought a jar of tea and a bowl of beans. I refused to eat. I shoved the food back at them, although the guard said I had to eat. I refused again. I nodded out from nerves and exhaustion but awoke when I heard the voice of a muezzin calling all the faithful to prayer.

The same guard came and secured me to a long shackle connected to the wall. I was alone in this room. They kept me here in solitary confinement, alone with my thoughts and my demons. Maybe they wanted me to break down, to crack and do their will. Sometimes I could hear them whispering behind the door.

Later, the guards brought me to the same room where I'd stood when I first arrived over a week ago. An older man in a neat military uniform sat majestically behind a desk, flanked by four armed gunmen. They did not wear uniforms. He spoke very precise English.

"Reverend, why are you here?" he asked me.

"I'm here to take Addie and the others home," I replied. "I've done everything you said. If you let us go, then we will fly home."

"Not so fast, infidel," the older man said. "Is that the only reason you came to Sudan? Some have said you're a government spy. Is that true?"

I was upset by that accusation. "Where do you get your information? I came here to see what was going on. I wanted to find out for myself. I heard terrible things, and I didn't want to believe the media's accounts."

"And now you are a part of those terrible things," the older man said, smiling. "You're spreading the gospel and the teachings of the Christ to blind the people. Why are you spreading this poison?"

My mouth was dry, and my heart was pounding. I knew what the older man was going to say next. The government man had warned me that they would want to recruit me.

But I interrupted him. "Where's Addie, my friend?"

A guard stepped up and hit me hard, sending stars and fog into my head. I collapsed, but then I stood up. Wobbly, I faced the older man, my eyes piercing. I was fed up with this game.

"Where's my friend?" I repeated.

The guard was about to strike me again, but the older man raised his hand. Luckily, these men were trained well, because there could have been trouble right then.

"Reverend, what we want from you is that you renounce your faith and your country," the older man said with a sneer on his lips. "If you do what we say, if you cooperate, you'll be freed before the weekend."

Being captive, I had no sense of time or place. What day was it? What week was it? What did it matter to me? The goal was to dangle a carrot before me, to give me false hope.

"Tell me about your associates at the camp," the older man said. "Give us some details. Prove to us that you want to be freed."

I was prepared for this chess game. "Why do you want to know, when you already know everything about the camp? We all know you have people working for you there. They're on to you big-time."

Another fist smashed into the back of my head. I almost blacked out, but I remained calm.

The older man nodded, and the guards went to work on me, punching and kicking me. They hurt me really badly, so badly that I passed out. I awoke in the cell, knowing I couldn't submit to these hostage takers. I wanted to strike a deal with them, the deal I had discussed with the bishop, but they had another agenda. If they got what they wanted, I would be left with nothing. No honor, no dignity, no pride, no faith.

35

THE SET-UP

When I awoke in that cell, I discovered two people in it with me, a man and a woman, both beaten and battered. They were dressed in ragged clothes that barely concealed their private parts, and their legs were bound by chains to the wall. I stirred, moving the chain binding my leg across the hard floor, causing them to open their eyes. Both of them were Sudanese. Both were the enemy of the rebels.

"Hello," I said, smiling a weak smile.

At first they didn't answer and just eyeballed me to size me up.

I braced myself against the wall; my head hurt very badly. Everyone had warned me constantly that these rebels meant business. I was totally baffled by what they wanted me to do. So far they had demanded that I renounce Christianity, just like Peter the Apostle denied Jesus twice, and that I renounce America and its freedom to worship. The older man was brutal; you could see it in his eyes. I endured terrible nightmares of being branded between my legs, of having my eyes and my tongue ripped out, my severed hands in a bucket of crimson water. The thought crossed my mind that nobody knew where I was. Possibly, the staffer hadn't told anyone. Or the guards. How could they find me? How could they rescue me?

"Who are you, sir?" the man asked in university English, proper and polite. "We're university students. They captured us and are holding us for ransom. These are cruel people."

"I'm Reverend Clint Winwood, an American who just came here to help out," I said, not really telling them why I had come.

"If you're Christian, you picked the wrong place to be," the woman said, covering her shattered mouth. "They kill ministers of the Christian faith here. They burn down churches and kill the followers."

The man scooted near the door, tugging his chain. "I'm Gatgong, and she's Marcy," he said by way of an introduction.

Marcy sniffed and spat on the floor. "We're both university students," she said. "We came down from Khartoum after the big protests. The authorities wanted to arrest me. We protested on campus after noon prayers, and we were tear-gassed by security forces. The security forces blocked all roads leading to the university after we threw rocks at them and burned tires to block streets. In response to us, the security forces fired live bullets. All around the city, protests continued, and the government cracked down on them, killing so many of us. They stormed into crowds, bashing protesters with batons and rifle butts, and assaulted even innocent bystanders."

"How did you get here?" I asked her.

Marcy wiped her eyes, about to cry. "I came down here from Khartoum," she said, sobbing. "The government has a deal with some of the militias. These people are getting arms and money from Khartoum. I came down to be with my family. They risked everything to hide me. An old girlfriend called the rebels and turned me in, so here I am."

"What are they charging you with?"

"Reverend, they don't have to charge us with anything," she replied.

Gatgong blurted out, "Some students contacted Amnesty International and the African Centre for Justice and Peace Studies. That really angered the government."

I looked closely at the dark man, with his broad nose, sharp features, and wiry body, while Marcy went on talking, her words tumbling out of her. He just watched and stared into space as she spoke.

"They're going to kill us," he said finally. "They don't want the ransom. They want to scare the young people so they will convert to Allah. We're as good as dead. We'll never get out of here. We will die in this miserable hole." Before he quieted, he talked about ending his life. There was nothing in the cell with which to commit suicide.

Foolishly, I didn't believe that. I comforted the two doubting young people with bits of scripture, but that got me only a savage beating with a whip of hard leather and a stern warning about spreading the word of the infidels. One of the guards had heard me reciting the Bible verses through the door. However, that didn't stop me.

"The Bible can give you great solace," I said, nursing a hard knot above my cheek. "In Second Timothy, two, fifteen, it says, 'Study to show thyself approved unto God, a workman that needeth not to be ashamed, rightly dividing the word of truth.' I love those verses."

In the days that followed, I often thought I was wasting my time trying to comfort them with the good book. Their only concern was survival.

You could tell this was a favorite holding pen for the rebels, with its mishmash of body smells, frenzied fingernail marks on the walls, blood stains from victims. Phantoms. There were plenty of ghosts in this cell. Between interrogations, I thought of my family life, my dead wife and the kids, the bittersweet days past. I also craved some contact with the outside world and freedom. So many thoughts were sandwiched between the harsh slaps, the angry shouts, and the questions. Sometimes the memories of my destroyed marriage moved me beyond my anxiety and sadness, transporting me far above this confused mess.

One afternoon, it was my turn for questioning. I accompanied the guards willingly, determined to keep silent. Another soldier, a stout man with a thick beard and dark glasses, had replaced the older man, whom I had found comforting in a strange way.

"Our leader made two simple requests of you, and I don't understand why you cannot fulfill them," the soldier said. "Renounce the Christian faith as the religion of infidels. Renounce your country as the sinful capital of evil and immoral acts. Why can't you do this?"

I kept silent. I glared at my captors defiantly.

"Why doesn't your God want everyone to be saved?" the soldier asked. "Why does He favor the rich and powerful? Why does He turn His back on others?"

I remained mute, but I maintained my hateful stare.

"Why doesn't your God love some and not others?" he asked sternly. "Answer that question. Why is your God so loving and compassionate, but He mistreats his followers with lives so full of suffering?"

I kept my mouth closed. Maybe my pleas to God for help were meaningless. Still, I continued them.

"Just renounce Jesus Christ and join the faith of Islam," the soldier said. "If you do not, you know you will die. There is no room in our faith for infidels."

I spat at the floor and shouted. "Islam is a religion of peace. Why do you pervert the religion of Allah?"

They stretched me out, facedown, one clutching my legs, the other holding my hands, and they took turns lashing me with a leather whip. Another one kicked me in the stomach and the privates. Then a soldier stood on my back, with the two men stretching me taut. They were not finished with me. They hoisted me up into the air by my feet, naked, and beat me cruelly on my butt and legs. The sharp pain sent me into numbness and blackness. They stopped when I lost consciousness.

About two hours later I awoke in the darkened cell. Flies surrounded my open wounds. They had beaten me to the point of exhaustion and death.

My faith in the Lord sustained me during my time of crisis. I remembered a favorite passage from the Bible, one that I had learned very early in my ministry. Ephesians 4:10–12 read: "He that descended is the same also that ascended up far above all heavens, that he might fill all things. And he gave some, apostles; and some, prophets; and some, evangelists; and some, pastors and teachers; For the perfecting of the saints, for the work of the ministry, for the edifying of the body of Christ."

I was feeling the network of bumps and bruises that covered the entire side of my face when the guards hurled Gatgong into the cell. The rebels had hacked his leg with a machete, creating a deep, jagged wound just below the knee. He was bleeding profusely. Quickly, Marcy and I sprang into action, putting a tourniquet, made from our remaining bits of clothing, on his leg. The bleeding soon stopped.

"They will kill us," he said. "Pray for us. We are dead people."

Marcy looked at me, thinking the same thing.

I prayed for us, asking the Lord to protect us. I asked Him to deliver us from this madness. I promised Him everything.

When I was finished, Marcy glanced at Gatgong, weeping softly. "I don't understand this kind of evil," she said. "In our district, they drove two cars with bombs into the big shopping area. One blast went off at the busiest time of the day for shopping. I saw it with my own eyes. The crowds ran, screaming and crying, away from the explosion. Then the second blast went off, killing the medics and burning the ambulances that had come to help the victims. What kind of people are these devils?"

"I don't know," I answered. "But this has nothing to do with religion. Not at all."

She continued to cry. "My mother died in my arms."

"Do either of you know Bishop Obote?" I asked them.

For once, Marcy stopped her tears. "I know him," she said, disregarding the cautionary looks from the injured Gatgong. "Although the bishop says he is a Christian, he is really a Muslim fundamentalist. He keeps the faith, praying five times a day, keeps the Ramadan fast, doesn't drink or smoke. He wears Western clothes and eats their food to fool the infidels."

I thought about how I had been duped by this man of goodwill in the Christian fellowship. Elsa had warned me about this man.

We took turns on the pot that served as a toilet. At first, I was nervous about letting them see me squat on the pot to relieve myself.

There was no privacy at all. Everybody saw everything we did. The smell of our cell was unbearable, thanks to our unwashed bodies, the uncontained human waste, the dirt and grime. What a horrible stench! Once a day, we were allowed to go outside for a few minutes and use a deep hole in the ground for toilet needs. A guard watched over us.

Once I was out in the open, I gazed at the sky, wishing I could soar into the heavens and be free. On bright mornings the sky was deep blue, like my heart.

At my next interrogation, with what seemed like my last ounce of strength, I punched the nearest guard in the head, and then I collapsed under a barrage of hard blows. They kept pummeling me until I blacked out.

The last thing I heard was a soldier say, "Forget it, Reverend. Jesus cannot help you here."

36

MAKE UP YOUR MIND

It was near the time of prayers. I knew something was up. The rebels had held a meeting for most of the night. I had listened to the scrambling of the soldiers in the hallway, armed and eager for battle. If the opportunity presented itself, I would run and not look back.

After our brief trip outside, the guards rushed into the cell and grabbed me forcefully. I had no power to resist. I was near the end of my rope. I had no willpower. As I passed them in the hallway, the soldiers talked about the destruction of a Christian church. A couple of bombs in the building, bricks in mounds from the blasts, the interior of the structure turned inside out, and pews out in the yard, near the road. Its pastor shot, and the church people running and dropping like birds at a bird shoot. Stained-glass windows crushed under the enemy's heels.

The older man was there this time when they dragged me into the big room. Under some strong questioning, I found myself having difficulty speaking. The words didn't come out. When I did talk, I stuttered painfully, and they laughed, laughed, laughed.

Laughing, the older man was handed a list of murdered ministers and a letter of approval from the government in the North. One of the rebels presented him with a trophy, a charred Bible from the destroyed church, and he examined it on the desk . They joked about how they had ordered four school-age girls to sing a hymn before they were lined up and shot.

"Here's what the newspapers say. 'The people who kill, rape, torture are cowards, and they will be treated as such," The older man read with gusto. "'They will pay a price, a very lofty price.'"

There was much rejoicing. As I sat there, in walked Bishop Obote, who greeted all those present and then took a seat near the older man. They were like old friends. They offered him something drink.

"You snake," I hissed at the bishop, who wore a blank expression.

"Greetings, Reverend. We meet in the strangest places," he said, grinning. "You probably thought you'd never see me again. I hope you're not disappointed in me."

"You walked me right into a trap," I replied.

I prayed that the good guys were following behind him. The locals didn't know we were in this building, but I had heard planes flying overhead. *Surveillance.*

"After the crisis in Darfur, I saw the suffering and decided to do anything to save my country," the bishop said. "I surrendered to God, and He told me that He would not choose any side. There was no right or wrong. I've done some bad things in my past. God's mercy washed that all away."

"You coward!" I shouted at him.

Everybody laughed at my puny insult, especially the older man.

"Do you want them to kill me?" I asked him loudly.

"No, I don't," the bishop said, fanning himself.

I clenched my fists, anger surging through me, hating how easily I'd been duped by a member of the Christian fellowship. This was not the first time. Just because someone said he loved the Lord didn't mean he followed scripture.

"I've been in your situation, back against the wall," the bishop said. "I've been beaten and lashed because of my faith. They ordered me to quit the church and convert to Islam. They ordered me to close my church and pledge my loyalty to their faith. Repent. Christianity is for foreigners, not Africans. If I decided to do this, everything would be given to me."

"There is no excuse for going over to the other side," I seethed. "People count on you. They look up to you. You're a liar. What's worse is that you lie to yourself."

"I'm not a politician," the bishop said, waving a hand. He turned to the older man and said, "Leave us. I want to talk to this man. Keep one of your men here so he won't escape. I want to talk some sense into his head."

They left, the bishop took the seat behind the desk, and we settled down to talk. I didn't trust anything he said. Elsa had warned me about this guy, who thought only about saving his own hide. He'd do anything to accomplish that goal.

"I'm a man of God," the bishop continued. "Even in your country, the good old United States, the clergy partners with politicians, such as Billy Graham. They keep the power and integrity of the church and get things done. I'm doing the same thing. Don't blame me. Don't judge me."

I had nothing for him but disgust.

The bishop was lecturing me about character, religion, faith.

"Reverend, the Sudanese people in the south are bound by traditional African religions, Islam, and Christianity," he explained. "You foreigners don't understand that mix. I love your devotion, your purity of faith. You're a good man, but you must change."

The freedom to worship was the obstacle in the War on Terror. Some on the other side said that theirs was the only way to worship God and that conflict was the only way to settle the question. I listened to the bishop and thought about how to escape.

"I preach the Christian gospel, but I'm prepared for any shift of power," the bishop said. "If any side wins, I win. The church has always been flexible and adaptable. You must be that way as well."

"No. I can't," I said.

The bishop laughed harshly. "Blessed are the peacemakers. . . . Turn the other cheek. . . . Love your enemy. The real world doesn't operate that way. As a Christian, you must be practical."

"The Lord died for all our sins," I said. "He died for all of us. You're a big sinner. Christians don't have to be two-faced. You can't serve the Lord and the devil. You cannot serve them both."

He put his feet up on the desk. "I know the biblical view of the sinner and all those lofty moral ideals go out the window when survival is involved. I'm not a savior. I'm a survivor. I'm thinking only of saving myself. You need to do likewise."

"I won't renounce my faith or my country," I replied.

"You need to think about what they're asking you to do," the bishop said. "I'm doing God's work, and you can too. Agree to their demands and be a free man."

It was my turn to laugh. "Do you think you are free? These people own you lock, stock, and barrel. You're their puppet."

"And you're going to die," the bishop said.

"Where's Addie?" I asked.

He changed the subject. "War is such a bad thing. It brings out the worst in people. I don't know why God allows such a thing as war, but it must serve a purpose."

"Where's Addie?" I repeated. "What's happened to her?"

"I thought you were finished with her," he said.

"How do you sleep nights?" I asked him.

The bishop's voice suddenly became strained. "Very solidly. As for your friend, government troops rescued her and the others. Your friend is safe."

"Is she really?" I asked. "Was she hurt?"

"One of her doctors told me that she suffered head injuries, a broken nose and ribs, and a fractured arm. She resisted them, fighting like a wildcat before they overcame her with force. She is in the hospital, recovering nicely."

I was grateful and sincerely happy that she was safe.

"I told them I would make you see the light," the bishop said. "You've got two days before you got to make up your mind. I've got to get your answer. Tell me you'll think about it."

"I will not." I wanted to spit in his face.

"I'll be back here, and you've got to give me your answer," he said, a grim expression on his face. "Time is running out. I won't be responsible for what happens to you."

The bishop called them back inside and told them to take me down to my cell. They tossed me down on its floor, battered and humiliated. Marcy and Gatgong looked at me suspiciously, like I was a bug crawling in somebody's dinner.

37

RUCKUS

The building shook to its foundation under the first mortar round. It knocked me down on my face. There was a series of gunfire outside. A guard unfastened our chains, motioned to us to get down. I wiped the perspiration from my face as I huddled near the door. Another blast took off a part of the roof, sending bricks and boards flying down the hallway.

"Flatten yourself against a wall," I shouted above the explosions. I didn't want to die here. I had to survive.

The attack had roused me from my sleep. Now, for the first time, I noticed that Gatgong had been maimed during my slumber. They had snipped off his fingers on both hands, but not his thumbs. Marcy had wrapped the bloody wounds with rags. He moaned and writhed from the pain of the mutilation.

Marcy held him, trying to soothe him. "We'll get out of here. Check the hall. See if the guards are out there."

I stuck out my head, looking for the enemy. The bullets ripped along the ceiling and the wall. I crawled to the right, waving to Marcy so that she followed me, and Gatgong stood up and ran in the opposite direction. He was cut down immediately.

"Keep down!" I yelled at Marcy.

One of the rebels near the door was awarded with a red spot on his forehead, followed by a hissing sound, and he dropped to the floor. Dead. The other rebel near the door returned fire at the darkness in the street.

"When we get a chance, run for it," I said to Marcy.

In an instant, several guns were firing at once, and there was total bedlam. The rebels were giving as good as they got. These were regulars, trained professionals, holy warriors. Still, they were getting picked off one by one.

"I'm scared, Reverend!" Marcy screamed. "Don't let me die."

It was out of my hands. I couldn't guarantee her safety. All I could hope was that these were friendlies coming to our rescue. This was a well-coordinated attack with maybe some of the same soldiers Elsa had promised me.

Hesitating for a moment after the second big explosion, I dived to the floor, with Marcy right behind me. My ears rang from the boom of the blast. I looked into a series of rooms, some small and others larger, and none of them were occupied by the rebels. I tried to keep my feet under me as the room tilted. I heard more shots. One rebel shouted, "Death to the infidels!" and then another and another. The gunfire increased as the rebels had chosen to make one last stand.

A soldier stood near a shattered window, shooting at flashes of automatic fire, trying to pick off the men who were running from tree to tree. The remaining rebels refused to run away from the fight, and they stood stock-still, shooting, their weapons jerking with each shot. Some of them were drenched with blood.

"Look here," I said, peeking out a window of one of the empty rooms as some of the rebels shot at our rescue team from the second story of a nearby building. The automatic fire bursts looked like the flashes of fireflies in the night. Marcy crawled to me and glanced at the eruption of violence.

Another explosion in the building knocked me down. I felt no pain. *Is this the way people die? Is this the end?* I thought. *I don't deserve to die like this.*

A rebel leveled his weapon and fired a burst through the doorway. I jumped him in the thick, dark smoke and wrestled him to the floor, trying all the while to yank the gun away from him. He pounded on my chest, pushing his fists hard against my body, growling angrily. In Arabic he chanted, "God is great. God is great. God is great." A shot sounded once, twice. I felt a stinging in my leg.

"Kill him! Kill him, Reverend!" Marcy shouted, leaping on the man, who had pinned me down. She bit his gun hand very hard.

For a moment, I thought of those holy warriors, the martyrs of their faith, whose dream was the reward of seventy-two virgins when they reached paradise.

The pistol rolled out of from his grasp. Marcy picked it up and fired a shot through the neck of the rebel. He shrieked and slumped to the floor on top of me.

I heard the rebels pushing furniture up to the windows, barricading themselves in place, determined to fight until the last man. From all accounts, these were men who would drop their weapons and surrender. The older man was pumping them up with tirades of battling the Great Satan and the worshippers of the infidel God. Sounds and smoke filled the air between the series of shots and explosions. I kept my head down. They started burning papers and documents and smashing a laptop computer with a hammer.

One of the men kept repeating, "There is no God but Allah, and Mohammed is His prophet."

Another true believer, one who had lectured me about how the Sudanese conflict resembled the Crusades, with the Christians against the Muslims, carried the stockpile of ammo and grenades to the basement. I heard his footsteps on the steps. The same man who had given me the history of Sudan's struggle, the religious and ethnic war, the civil wars between the North and the South, Arabs against Africans, Muslims against Christians. He had bragged to me about how brutal the rebels had been when they'd gone door to door in the village, searching for informers and Christians. I tensed up, fearing an explosion from below that would kill us all.

The smoke was getting very thick in the rooms. My lungs ached, and my legs ached. The friendlies had arrived, and they were pouring into the backyard, shooting everything in sight, coming into the building.

"Follow me," I said, guiding the woman through the blinding air. A mercenary soldier found us and led us out into the open.

Three more shells were targeted at the main room of the building, and small blasts could be heard from where we lay in the yard. Gunfire sounded over and over. The survivors on the rebel side fled into the bush.

One of the mercenaries was talking on a radio. He was calling in a report. "The captives are safe. Repeat, the captives are safe," he said.

38

THE WHOLE WIDE WORLD IN HIS HANDS

It took me several weeks to locate Addie. An aide for the Sudanese government drove me to the local make-shift hospital where she was recovering. When I pulled up, she was sitting in the shade of a tree, surrounded by doctors and volunteers. Several photographers and reporters were gathered around her, too, and they were shouting questions and snapping her picture. Her face was strangely blank, her eyes were dead and lifeless, and she looked slightly frail. I stood there, just out of her sight.

Somebody had made her up, putting some eye shadow and bright red lipstick on her. Her hair was done in an odd fashion and was not in her usual style. She wore a plain hospital frock, and her feet were bare.

As I walked toward the group, I looked back at the collection of tents that provided emergency medical care at the hospital and saw the staffers hurrying in and out, the trucks pulling up with precious cargo.

"How soon will she be able to go home?" I asked a nurse.

She replied, "Any day now. As soon as the doctors think she can stand the long flight home." She paused. "There are other things wrong with her, other than her physical ailments," she added.

"What do you mean?" I asked.

The nurse spoke slowly. "While your friend was being held hostage, she was sexually assaulted. Five rebels held her hands and feet and took turns. They did this to her for over four hours. When we found her, she couldn't walk. She was hemorrhaging."

"Oh, my God! I . . . I . . . I . . ." I was stunned.

"How well do you know her?" she asked me.

"I know her very well," I answered. "What can I do?"

She folded her arms and put on a concerned face. "She doesn't remember a lot of her assault. We learned some of the facts from another captive who was there with her. You must see that she gets help when she gets stateside."

I nodded, still reeling from the bad news.

After I asked her a dumb question, about why rape was a weapon in this war, she told me that rape was considered the spoils of conflict. Rape was used to dehumanize the enemy. In this case, rape was used to dehumanize a tomboyish country gal from Alabama who didn't know the score or the players over here. She was considered collateral damage, something that just happened.

"She keeps saying she wishes she had died that night," the nurse said. "She feels guilty and ashamed."

"I can understand that," I replied.

"A bright spot is that she considers herself lucky because she tested negative for HIV," she said. "That would have been a real problem, especially since she's expecting."

"A baby?" I was totally shocked.

"She'll need a very good support network, along with some counseling for her emotional trauma," she remarked.

I had prayed that Addie would return to life, that she would be alive. Nothing had prepared me for these circumstances. The nurse told me that a doctor had advised Addie to "forgive and forget" what had happened to her.

How could she do that? I didn't know how she could do this, especially when she had the baby. The baby would serve as a reminder of the sexual violence committed against her.

"It's an outrage and a tragedy," the nurse said, summing it up. "But this is what happens to thousands of African women every day. They have to live with the scourge of rape. Usually, they have nobody to turn to for counseling or advice."

I waited for all the media to leave Addie's side. She sat there after they were gone, staring into space. Quietly, I moved down the slope to her. When I got within arm's reach, I touched her slightly. She flinched and turned to see that it was me. I knelt by her and talked softly.

"How are you, Addie?" I asked. "I missed you."

"I'm alive," she said solemnly.

"I'm glad you are," I replied. "But how are you feeling?"

She took my hand tenderly in hers and pulled it to her. She leaned forward, her eyes suddenly shut, and was oddly still.

"You came back for me," she said quietly. "You care, after all." She was silent for a moment. "I gave you a hard time, didn't I?"

"Not really," I lied.

Her voice was tight. "I told them I was a Christian, and they raped me."

"I know, Addie." A chill surged through me.

"I'm no longer afraid," she said, the words low and strong. "I no longer doubt myself. I no longer feel like I failed. I no longer believe what people say about me. I've faced the most horrible thing that can happen to a woman, and I lived."

"I'm glad about that," I said. "But you'll need help."

"I sure will," she replied. "I'm having a baby. Two of the nurses advised me to abort it. They said it could make me only more depressed."

"A baby is more than a notion," I said. "You should be sure."

That perked her up. "I was born a woman, black, and poor. All strikes against me, like most women in the black South. I've had to fight to get people to take me seriously."

"You should take your time before you made that decision," I said.

"I already know what I'll do, Reverend. Also, thank you for trying to rescue me. I heard how hard you tried."

"A child is for life," I replied, going back to her pregnancy. "You can't take it back and return it to the store. It's a big responsibility."

"Are you trying to talk me out of this?"

"No, I'm not."

She looked at me like she was trying to read my heart. I believed she wanted to know whether I was going to stick with her. She was the bravest woman I knew. For her courage, I was no longer afraid to take the plunge. It was not that I felt sorry for her. She would need my care, support, and love in the days to come. She was a broken soul, but she could heal.

I knew the Lord's mercy healed. I honored that miracles could happen. She was a warrior. I didn't know how right I was about her. But time would tell.

UC HIS GLORY BOOK CLUB!

www.uchisglorybookclub.net

UC His Glory Book Club is the spirit-inspired brain-child of Joylynn Ross, an author and the acquisitions editor of Urban Christian, and Kendra Norman-Bellamy, an author for Urban Christian. It is an online book club that hosts authors of Urban Christian. We welcome as members all men and women who have a passion for reading Christian-based fiction.

UC His Glory Book Club pledges its commitment to providing support, positive feedback, encouragement, and a forum whereby members can openly discuss and review the literary works of Urban Christian authors.

There is no membership fee associated with UC His Glory Book Club;however, we do ask that you support the authors by purchasing their works, encouraging them, providing book reviews, and, of course, offering your prayers. We also ask that you respect our beliefs and follow the guidelines of the book club. We hope to receive your valuable input, opinions, and reviews that build up, rather than tear down, our authors.

What We Believe:

—We believe that Jesus is the Christ, Son of the Living God.

—We believe that the Bible is the true, living Word of God.

—We believe that all Urban Christian authors should use their God-given writing ability to honor God and to share the message of the written word that God has given to each of them uniquely.

—We believe in supporting Urban Christian authors in their literary endeavors by reading their titles, purchasing them, and sharing them with our online community.

—We believe that everything we do in our literary arena should be done in a manner that will lead to God being glorified and honored.

We look forward to online fellowship with you.

Please visit us often at:

www.uchisglorybookclub.net

Many Blessings to You!

Shelia E. Lipsey,
President, UC His Glory Book Club

ORDER FORM
URBAN BOOKS, LLC
97 N18th Street
Wyandanch, NY 11798

Name (please print):_____

Address: _____

City/State: _____

Zip: _____

QTY	TITLES	PRICE

Shipping and handling: add $3.50 for 1st book, then $1.75 for each additional book.

Please send a check payable to:

Urban Books, LLC

Please allow 4-6 weeks for delivery

ORDER FORM
URBAN BOOKS, LLC
97 N18th Street
Wyandanch, NY 11798

Name (please print):_____

Address: _____

City/State: _____

Zip: _____

QTY	TITLES	PRICE
	3:57 A.M Timing Is Everything	$14.95
	A Man's Worth	$14.95
	A Woman's Worth	$14.95
	Abundant Rain	$14.95
	After The Feeling	$14.95
	Amaryllis	$14.95
	An Inconvenient Friend	$14.95
	Battle of Jericho	$14.95
	Be Careful What You Pray For	$14.95
	Beautiful Ugly	$14.95
	Been There Prayed That:	$14.95
	Before Redemption	$14.95

Shipping and handling-add $3.50 for 1st book, then $1.75 for each additional book.

Please send a check payable to:

Urban Books, LLC

Please allow 4-6 weeks for delivery

ORDER FORM
URBAN BOOKS, LLC
97 N18th Street
Wyandanch, NY 11798

Name(please print):_____

Address: _____

City/State: _____

Zip: _____

QTY	TITLES	PRICE
	By the Grace of God	$14.95
	Confessions Of A Preachers Wife	$14.95
	Dance Into Destiny	$14.95
	Deliver Me From My Enemies	$14.95
	Desperate Decisions	$14.95
	Divorcing the Devil	$14.95
	Faith	$14.95
	First Comes Love	$14.95
	Flaws and All	$14.95
	Forgiven	$14.95
	Former Rain	$14.95
	Humbled	$14.95

Shipping and handling-add $3.50 for 1st book, then $1.75 for each additional book.

Please send a check payable to:

Urban Books, LLC

Please allow 4-6 weeks for delivery

ORDER FORM
URBAN BOOKS, LLC
97 N18th Street
Wyandanch, NY 11798

Name (please print):_____

Address: _____

City/State: _____

Zip: _____

QTY	TITLES	PRICE
	From Sinner To Saint	$14.95
	From The Extreme	$14.95
	God Is In Love With You	$14.95
	God Speaks To Me	$14.95
	Grace And Mercy	$14.95
	Guilty Of Love	$14.95
	Happily Ever Now	$14.95
	Heaven Bound	$14.95
	His Grace His Mercy	$14.95
	His Woman His Wife His Widow	$14.95
	Illusions	$14.95
	In Green Pastures	$14.95

Shipping and handling-add $3.50 for 1st book, then $1.75 for each additional book.

Please send a check payable to:

Urban Books, LLC

Please allow 4-6 weeks for delivery

ORDER FORM
URBAN BOOKS, LLC
97 N18th Street
Wyandanch, NY 11798

Name: (please print): _____

Address: _____

City/State: _____

Zip: _____

QTY	TITLES	PRICE
	Into Each Life	$14.95
	Keep Your enemies Closer	$14.95
	Keeping Misery Company	$14.95
	Latter Rain	$14.95
	Living Consequences	$14.95
	Living Right On Wrong Street	$14.95
	Losing It	$14.95
	Losing Hope	$14.95
	Marriage Mayhem	$14.95
	Me, Myself and Him	$14.95
	Murder Through The Grapevine	$14.95
	My Father's House	$14.95

Shipping and handling-add $3.50 for 1st book, then $1.75 for each additional book.

Please send a check payable to:

Urban Books, LLC

Please allow 4-6 weeks for delivery

ORDER FORM
URBAN BOOKS, LLC
97 N18th Street
Wyandanch, NY 11798

Name: (please print):_____

Address: _____

City/State: _____

Zip: _____

QTY	TITLES	PRICE
	My Mother's Child	$14.95
	My Son's Ex Wife	$14.95
	My Son's Wife	$14.95
	My Soul Cries Out	$14.95
	Not Guilty Of Love	$14.95
	Prodigal	$14.95
	Rain Storm	$14.95
	Redemption Lake	$14.95
	Right Package, Wrong Baggage	$14.95
	Sacrifices of Joy	$14.95
	Secret Place	$14.95
	Without Faith	$14.95

Shipping and handling-add $3.50 for 1st book, then $1.75 for each additional book.

Please send a check payable to:

Urban Books, LLC

Please allow 4-6 weeks for delivery